Taking Names

a Type N sequel

Michelle N. Onuorah

Taking Names
Published by MNO Media, LLC
Printed in the U.S.A.

Printed Edition ISBN-13: 978-0692304266
Printed Edition ISBN-10: 0692304266

Please note there is occasional cursing, violence, and various references to
sexuality and spirituality within this work of fiction. Reader discretion is
advised.

Praise for Type N

"Can you imagine being the CURE ALL for all types of disease and problems? Can you imagine going from the NOBODY, that every one over looks and forgets is there, to the major SOMEBODY that no one will leave alone? If you want a book that's: fast paced, starts off right from page one in to the thick of things, a twist, betrayal, murder, quick resolution, holds your attention from the get go, and a little romance thrown in to a unique story, then look no further."

-Jenn Morgan, leader of New Adult Corner Book Club

"Type N is a gripping read with the perfect ending."

-Kira Watson, blogger of My Dear Bibliophage

"Well-crafted and exquisitely written, Type N is definitely a page turner. From the first page to the last, Michelle had me hooked to the story with grips of steel. This book receives five stars from me for getting my attention and never letting go. It opened my eyes to the many possibilities in this world. The intricate layers composed of faith and fate add to the equanimity of this novel. From religious readers to fiction lovers, this book is a must-read for everyone. I highly recommend this book!"

-Harold Ekeh

"Wow. Just wow. I loved this book. Absolutely love this book. This first read book made me see a whole new side to the world... Michelle N. Onuorah puts you in a speeding jet that goes into a tailspin and crashing to earth...You will never see the government the same again. This novel truly is an example of human nature and the will to survive...This book gets straight to the point and never slows down. You will be hooked from the first page, so be ready for the ride."

-Danielle Wilson

"If you enjoy the writing styles of Stephanie Meyers or Orson Scott Card I highly recommend Type N. Ms. Onuorah skillfully engages her readers by introducing you to a relatable protagonist that has been blessed or cursed with an incredible world changing ability. She deftly and honestly engages moral ethical struggles, burgeoning theology, and a blossoming relationship that leaves the reader wishing for more. Her character development is much appreciated in a time where authors seem to care more about flash and dazzle then substance. The only criticism I have is that I wish there was more. I definitely see this book easily adaptable to film because the dialogue, character development, and story are already served up!"

-Micah Lemon

"While reading, I could feel the tension between characters and connected with the protagonist right away. Without giving too much away, there was one part that had me pacing the room worried about the characters. The book isn't all action, there is some good relief that will make you smile and laugh…"

-Dannica June Anderson

"A must read - it needs to be made into a movie! There is action and romance and it's just a really awesome story! The book was so much on my mind that I dreamed of Nikki and Jason all morning! Got up at nine and finished it quickly!"

-Lisa (Moon) White

Other Titles by Michelle N. Onuorah

Type N
Remember Me
Double Identity
Wanna Be on Top?

Available online at Amazon, Barnes & Noble, Kobo, and other stores

ACKNOWLEDGMENTS

I want to thank Dr. Victoria Oshodi for undertaking the daunting task of editing this novel. I would also like to thank Karla Henderson for serving as my beta reader. Both of you were invaluable to the development of this sequel.

Author's Note

This novel is a part of a series and is not intended to be read independently of the first novel, *Type N*. I **strongly** recommend that you read that novel prior to reading this one - otherwise it might not make much sense to you.

CHAPTER ONE

Moscow, Russia – 12:00 PM

Nicolette:

My left shoulder is sore. I'm worried that I've broken a bone or wrenched a socket in the landing. I need to get out of here. Shortly after my insane jump, the truck exits the freeway and pulls into a busy shopping center. As he drives through an outside parking lot, I climb out of the cab, hang off the end of the truck and jump off. It drives on. I get strange glances from strangers but by some miracle, the driver doesn't detect me.

My shoulder is on fire now and my whole arm feels numb. Something is wrong. I rush into what looks like a convenience store and immediately catch the attention of the employees there. They don't say anything but they look at me strangely, not in recognition but concern at my pained expression and the way I'm gripping my arm. I probably look disheveled too.

"First aid," I say in Russian. One of the reps points to aisle four. I stride to it, pull the first kit I find, tuck it under my right arm and quickly slam more than enough money on the counter top with my right hand. I turn to the bathroom at the back of the store before the attendants can even speak. The minute I close the door, I strip off my backpack, jacket, and shirt. First things first. I place a firm hand on my left shoulder, take a deep breath and wrench it back into place. The pain is blinding and the shock of it knocks the breath out of me. My gasps fill the bathroom.

Whatever relief I feel in having my shoulder back in place is suspended when I look at it in the mirror. Immediately, I see another problem.

There is something implanted in my shoulder and dried blood has streaked from the entry site. I push and prod at it and then realize – it's a *bullet.* I've never seen this before and feel like the subject of a strange sci-fi show. The dried streak of blood around my wound indicates that I bled but only briefly. The wound is closed around the bullet. My skin stitched itself back together over a wound that would ordinarily require stitches at the least. But I can't leave it like that. Even if I don't get an infection from the foreign object, the feel of it there is incredibly uncomfortable.

I have to get it out.

I wash my hands, open the kit, pull on gloves, and immediately go for the scalpel. I sterilize it then force myself to do what I would normally find nauseating. I swallow my fear and dig the edge of the blade into my skin. Ignoring the blood, I cut a small circle around the edge of the bullet, and dig into the new opening. I dig and push as blood streams past my shoulder and onto my chest. The tip of the blade makes contact with the bullet. I pry it out and hear it clink into the bowl of the sink. I check around the burrow of the wound for any shrapnel pieces. It's clear. Red but clear. I bite my lip and hold back a scream as I sterilize the wound with alcohol, pack it with gauze, and seal it with tape. I hope it will close on its own again. Otherwise, the stitching will have to wait.

I've got to get out of here.

I toss the contents of the rudimentary surgery away and clean myself up. My clothes are ruined with blood and I think that's what alarmed the employees the most. I change tops but wear the same jacket.

As I emerge from the bathroom, I can tell something is up. There are whispers in Russian. I walk down an aisle concealing myself from sight of the employees at the front desk. Through cans of shaving cream and deodorant, I see them. Three men in *politsiya* uniforms. I don't have time for this. I walk to the end of the aisle and make myself visible. The three men straighten and I see recognition flash in their eyes. One pulls his radio to his mouth. The other says, "Excuse me, ma'am," in Russian. I ignore him and turn into another aisle. I hear their feet scatter. I stride down one aisle and hear them stride down the one parallel to me on my left. I glance at the corner ceilings and, just as I expected, find large mirrors stationed on every corner of the building. I grab a can of what appears to be hair spray and pop off the cap. Stand at the end of the aisle and watch as one of the men bound down to my direction.

"Aminev," a *politsiya* suddenly yells in warning. He's seen the mirror and so does my target. Aminev reaches for his gun but I'm quicker. I knock his hand with the edge of my foot, strike the side of his head with my forearm and stomp my foot in my favorite place on the knee. He crumples to the ground and I quickly disarm him. I hold my hand steady and shoot out the mirrors. First one, then another, until all four are blown out. I barely hear the screams of customers as they race out of the building in a mad dash. I yank up Aminev by his uniform and plant the barrel of my gun into his dark hair.

His partners have no choice but to face me. Their guns drawn, they see they're at a disadvantage as their comrade lies in clear hostage. They come from separate corners but I can see them both. I look at the cop on my left and gesture to the cop on the right.

"Join him," I command in Russian. His eyebrows shoot up in surprise at my use of the language. He slowly moves to join the other officer.

I'm calling the shots now.

Kuchchaveli Beach, Sri Lanka – Five Weeks Earlier:

I breathe deep. Hold the breath and feel the rush of liquid as I submerge beneath the water. It's still. Warm at the surface, cool down below. The sun beams forth, warming my face. It's nothing compared to the warmth in my heart. Time stands still under that water and all I hear is liquid silence. Peace below. I meet Him in the deep and it blows my mind that centuries ago, He did the very same thing. He leaned back into the water, His back held by His cousin. He broke through the water and felt the sun dance off the droplets on His face. This isn't just a ritual. Or a ceremony. It's a celebration. Of the life I have in Him. My God. My Christ. My baptism.

I break through the water. The cheers are overwhelming. No dove descends and the sky doesn't part but I know that He is pleased. I know I am His child. I believe that Jesus Christ is all that he claimed to be and I know that He lives. I don't know exactly when I started to believe. I think maybe I always did - even as a kid. But I didn't know how to connect with Him until Isaiah and Jason showed me how. And I didn't admit it until Jason asked.

I open my eyes and look at Jason. The man who introduced me to my Savior. The man who gave up everything to keep me safe. The man who told me he loved me just hours after we escaped. There are tears in his dark blue eyes but they come from nothing short of joy. Nothing short of love. Finally, we can be one. Our new beginning is limitless.

Jason:

This has to be the most unusual baptism-wedding to ever take place. The fact that it's a baptism-wedding is strange in and of itself.

And yet it's right.

When Nic breaks through the water, a joy and a peace so potent overtakes us all. I cheer, Pastor Thennakoon cheers and so do the members of his small congregation - our fellow Brothers and Sisters. There are no more than six people in the water with us. She turns to me immediately and I wrap her up in my arms, soaking right along with her. I think back to the lonely, sullen teenager I first met nearly three years ago. When she was dressed in nothing but black and had no one to call friend. She has transformed. Always beautiful, God's light shines in her and through her. Her jet black hair glistens in the sun and her skin glows with a healthy tan. Her cheeks are flushed with excitement. Her smile is radiant and it makes her all the more beautiful to me.

One year. More than a year, actually.

It's been more than a year since I first told Nic I loved her on that charter plane. I have waited - honoring her with my patience; refusing to push her into anything she wasn't ready for: a deeper relationship with me, which would only happen with a deeper relationship with God. She accepted Christ into her heart only months after we arrived in Sri Lanka but she waited to get baptized. And I waited to propose. The baptism is over. I'm ready for the wedding.

We turn to face the pastor. We're both drenched in water as we stand waist deep in the sea. She wears a simple white dress and I match her with a simple white collared shirt. My khakis cling to my legs under water but I don't mind. Pastor Thennakoon reaches to one of the congregants and they pass him a leather-back Bible. He's careful to hold it high above the water as he reads:

"'A man will leave his father and mother and be united to his wife, and they will become one flesh.' We are gathered here today to join this man and this woman into holy matrimony under the witness and blessing of God."

He says it again in *Sinhala*.

Nic and I join hands. We're still drenched. There's no makeup, no videographer, no frills or thrills associated with the typical Western wedding. But it doesn't matter. We're not in the West and we no longer need the frills. There is love; our love for each other and more importantly, our love for the One uniting us. She's radiant - more beautiful to me than she ever was before. We exchange the vows in English but speak very low. So low that only Pastor Thennakoon can hear what we're saying:

"I, Jason Dockery Monroe, take you, Nicolette Jennifer Talloway, to be my lawfully wedded wife. To have and to hold from this day forward, for better or worse, for richer or poorer, in sickness and in health."

Tears flow freely down her cheeks as I meet her eyes and pledge my life to her.

"I vow to love, honor, and cherish you. In the name of Jesus Christ, I commit my heart and my body to you and to our marriage and I pledge to you my fidelity until death do us part."

Our rings are simple golden bands - hers, slim and feminine; mine, slightly thicker. I slip hers on and kiss it as it beams brightly on her hand.

A smile breaks through the tears as she squeezes my hands and mouths "I love you." I immediately mouth it back.

It's her turn.

She takes a deep breath and steadies herself. Meets my eyes again and begins:

"I, Nicolette Jennifer Talloway, take you, Jason Dockery Monroe, to be my lawfully wedded husband. To have and to hold from this day forward, for better or worse, for richer or poorer." Her voice breaks and she pauses, tears gushing forth again. My own have long since fallen.

She continues, "In sickness and in health. I vow to love, honor, and cherish you. In the name of Jesus Christ, I commit my heart and my body to you and our marriage. I pledge to you my fidelity until death do us part."

She slips the band on my finger and I look at it. I raise my eyes to hers and am held hostage by her eyes.

We're all silent for a moment. We hear nothing but the waves as the words sink in to both of us - the commitment we just made to one another - that we'll hold ourselves to for the rest of our lives. I'm not afraid. I've been ready for so long. All I feel is a happiness I never thought I could feel. Suddenly, Pastor Thennakoon's voice booms out in *Sinhala*:

"I now pronounce you Mr. and Mrs. Oliver Smith!"

The church cheers and claps as Pastor Thennakoon smiles mischievously at us. He's the only one who knows, the only one we've trusted enough to tell and he's kept our confidence for the past year. All of our documents read "Dr. Oliver Smith" and "Jennifer Dawson." Even the marriage license we filed yesterday. In the eyes of the church members, the public, and the Sri Lankan government, Nic and I are two people who don't really exist. We can let it bother us or we can accept it as a price to pay for our freedom. Besides, God knows the truth. The vows that we just gave were the truth. Pastor Thennakoon knows this too. He looks at us and whispers in English:

"I now pronounce you Dr. and Mrs. Jason Monroe." He looks at me. "You may kiss your lovely bride."

I turn my focus back to her and all I can see are her hazel eyes. They're glowing with elation, love, and a fearless anticipation for the life we have ahead of us. I pull Nic flush into my arms, cradle her gently at the nape of her neck and lower my mouth to hers. The cheers from the crowd thunder in my ears as we kiss. Her lips are soft, wet, and inviting. I get so lost in the moment it takes me a second to realize we're not alone.

"Hey, hey - save some for your wedding night!" Pastor Thennakoon teases in *Sinhala*. The crowd roars in laughter.

I pull back blushing but Nic just laughs. She catches my eye and begins to sober.

We're married.

Nicolette:

Finally.

I have been waiting for this night for so long. The reception is over, Pastor Thennakoon and the rest of our guests have gone home. The sun is just setting as Jason and I stand in what was once his room. For over a year we've lived in separate small beach houses only yards away from each other, right by the water. Jason had been intent on finding separate homes that wouldn't lend us to compromising his values; values that soon became mine.

But that season is over. We're married now. And our homes will now converge into one.

We face each other. It's times like this that I can't get past how beautiful he is. It's like God was in a really good mood the day He made him and rather than just painting a decent picture, He decided to create a masterpiece out of him. The setting sun casts a warm orange-pink glow on the side of my new husband's face. His hair is blonder than it ever was. He keeps it cropped but it's longer than it was in the States and is tousled from the day's activities. I blush to think how much more tousled it's about to get. The shadows cast by the mellow sun sharpen the angles of his high cheekbones, chiseled jaw, and perfect straight nose. But it's his eyes…his eyes give me chills. The dark blue set against the warm orange glow of the sun. And they're fixed on me with a look I've only glimpsed once or twice in all our time together. They're hungry with an intensity that makes my senses swim.

He desires me.

And I desire him.

I slowly kick off the sandals on my feet. Remove the bangle from my wrist and let it drop to the floor with a careless thud. Finally, I remove the straps of my dress. It falls to a puddle at my feet. I hear his sharp intake of breath. He echoes my movements. Removes his sandals, his shirt and his pants. We stand in front of each other, only covered by underwear. I'm barely aware of the breath that comes out as a gasp. What's wrong with me? I've seen magazine covers and movie posters before. I've seen shirtless actors with ripped bodies. Heck, I've seen

Jason without his shirt on before, swimming at the beach. But there's something different about seeing Jason shirtless before me right now, in this moment. Knowing that his body, taut with muscle, is for me and me alone. I look back up into his eyes and see the same look of awe reflected back at me. His breath has accelerated and is quicker than my own.

He steps forward. Takes my hand and places it on his warm chest in invitation. I accept it and allow my hands to explore the planes of his hard muscled chest, shoulders, biceps, and torso. I can feel his heart racing. He feels so strong, almost imposing as he towers over me. The thought of being intimate with him is almost intimidating. He must read it on my face.

"Don't be afraid. I'll be gentle."

I smile up at him, at his look of concern for me.

"I know you will," I reply.

I take his hands and bring them to my waist in invitation. He steps closer and caresses my back and shoulders. He looks down at me, cherishing me, assessing my readiness. I meet his eyes and nod. He lowers his mouth to mine and kisses all the thoughts away. Kisses me until I hardly notice when we reach the bed. Kisses me until it barely registers that all our clothes are gone.

He is gentle.

And patient. He's a selfless lover and I'm the beneficiary. And though my body feels the pain of him taking my virginity, it thrills me to see the pleasure register on his face. He doesn't let it cloud him from focusing on me. He watches me closely, his dark blue eyes gauging my expression as he loves me tenderly. And as he loves me tenderly, the pain recedes to the background and a new pleasure springs forth. Our breaths mingle as we give, we take, and we enjoy our union. He makes me his wife and I make him my husband.

Our covenant is consummated. We've finally become one.

Jason:

My body burned with a thirst only she could quench. And she's quenched it. The only flame that's left in me is one that settles deep in

I kick. Propel myself forward as a lightheaded sensation takes over. I need oxygen. I'm at my very last end. I race forward and kick harder. There's a large shadow just ahead and I need to reach it if I have any chance of leaving unspotted.

I make it. Kick up - and burst forth above the water. I gasp in relief as the air fills my lungs. But I can't stop. I have to keep going. I'm right under the parallel bridge and I can hear an agent jump into the water a few yards away. All the attention is focused around the other bridge. I swim ashore, strip off my shirt, and power walk into the crowd. I look like just another beach goer, walking around after a swim. I turn the corner past visibility and finally run. Jason had all of our money with him. I have to go back.

I ignore the glances, ignore the stares as I race my way back to the cottage.

Nothing prepares me.

Nothing prepares me for the shock of stepping into our home. It's bright and cool inside. The curtains flutter against the beach breeze and the salty air fills the quiet home. Our knick knacks are just where we left them. Jason's planner sits open at his desk, right on top, there's a photo. The one he was trying to tell me about. I pick it up with trembling hands and finally take a look. It's the two of us, waist deep in water, staring at each other as Pastor Thennakoon speaks. The sun shines brightly and reflects off of the water and there's joy all around us but we're not paying attention. We only have eyes for each other. That day rushes back to me but so does the sight of his blood. I stumble back. My legs hit the edge of the bed and I sag against it. I look around, shocked. I'm sitting on the bed we once shared together. The bed we made love on just hours ago. I never thought it would be the last time. Our home sits in perfect peace, the water lapping up against the nearby shore like everything is normal. It doesn't know. It doesn't know that everything has been tainted. Everything is gone. Ruined.

He's gone.

The room swims as the tears well. They burn the back of my eyes but don't compare to the pain in my chest. I cling to the sheets beneath me and fold over. Suddenly, I can't breathe. The sobs rack my body as they rumble low and deep. I just held him. He was just here. He's gone.

I'm scared now. The air isn't coming in. My lungs are threatening to take me to the grave right along with him but part of me wants them to.

I don't want to live. Not without him. Lord, I don't want to live.

His face flashes before me. His eyes the deepest blue. I can see his smile. Smell his skin. Hear his deep laugh. He could have escaped but he didn't. He stayed - and died - for me.

What would his death mean if I simply died along with him?

He can't die in vain. The breath returns. My lungs fill up again. And suddenly, the tears begin to slow down. I have to get out of here. This isn't over. I barrel over to the closet and change. I rip off my wet clothes, change into fresh bottoms, and pull on a fitted tank top. I pull one of Jason's sweaters and wrap it around my waist. I grab his baseball cap and yank it on my head, pulling it close to my eyes. Next, I yank out a backpack and throw items in it. I start to think in lists. Clothes? Check. Cash? Check. Laptop? Check. Guns? Check. I shove all of my ID into the bag - his too. I'll burn it later. I fold the photo and tuck it into my pocket. I can't lose it. It's the last of him I have. Everything essential is packed. I can catch the ferry in half an hour but I have to move. I throw the backpack on, look around the room one last time, and stride out to the front door.

I know I'll never see this place again.

CHAPTER THREE

Nicolette:

Seconds turn into minutes, minutes turn into hours and hours take me further and further away from the last moment Jason was alive. I'm not living. I'm functioning. I operate on autopilot when I take the ferry from Sri Lanka to India and then board the flight from Madurai to Moscow. The flight is six and a half hours. I watch the clock like a mad woman, dreading every minute that passes, every time the long hand hits the twelve. It signals the passage of another hour.

Time waits for no man and like clockwork, I remind myself.

Two hours ago, he was alive.

Three hours ago, he was alive.

Four hours ago, he could talk to me.

Twelve hours ago, he held me in bed.

I can't sleep. Every time I try to close my eyes, I see him on that bridge, soaked in blood, panting against the pain, desperately pleading for me to leave and let them take him instead.

I didn't get to say goodbye. I didn't even get to bury him. The thought of him dead, his body floating somewhere in a river in a foreign country... I swallow hard and push back the tears. I keep reciting the incident over and over in my mind. What could I have done differently? I should have found a way to take them both on. I should have let him keep the gun. I never should have run ahead of him in the first place. Maybe if we had been right next to each other, they wouldn't have tried to shoot. I should have agreed with him and moved ahead of time, when the news report first came out.

You should have left him out of it when they killed your parents.

I close my eyes at the accusatory thought. Tears burn behind my eyelids. It's true. Had I left him alone or ran with Natalia and Nate, he would still be alive in Washington state, practicing medicine and living his life. He was only twenty-two. Up until this moment, the worst pain I ever felt was losing my parents over a year ago for the same thing - my blood. But this feels even worse than their loss. The man I became one with is now dead and in his death, I have died too.

I reach into my pocket and pull out the picture. I think back to him looking at the same photo and almost feel closer to him at the mere thought. I can't remember the look in his eyes as he held it. I had been too busy, running around getting ready for a stupid class. For all my practicing and training, it did nothing to save the one who mattered most to me. I look at the photo. The way he looks at me in it. No one will ever love me the way he did. No one will ever *see* me the way he did.

Where is he now? Not his body but *him*.

A past conversation comes to mind and I lose myself in the memory.

"Do you believe in hell?" I ask.

He nods.

"How do you know where you're going?"

"Once I accepted Christ, I was destined for heaven."

He sounds so sure. So positive. For a few moments we're both quiet. I pick up the conversation on a different track this time.

"You've given up a lot for me," I begin.

He shakes his head.

"Enough about me," he says. "Tell me more about your life growing up. Who were your friends?"

I grow uncomfortable.

"I don't have any friends."

I let the admission hang dead in the air and stare at the rolling wheat fields that pass us outside.

"Why not?" he asks in a very serious tone.

I know he can tell I don't want to talk about this. But he pushes me anyway.

"Can I be honest with you?" he asks. "I noticed you in the hospital. The night of your brother's accident. I noticed that you weren't talking to anyone and they weren't talking to you."

"So you noticed that I was a weirdo –"

"Absolutely not," he says. "I noticed that the people around you were inconsiderate jerks who didn't have the decency to try and comfort you during such a difficult time."

I look at him and can see the flare of anger in his eyes and it bowls me over. Maybe I'm not crazy. Maybe my isolation isn't entirely my fault. I think about my mom's letter to me and recognize that she and Dad made a choice too. When I withdrew, they chose not to engage with me. They chose to let me be. And so did everyone else around me. Whether or not I withdrew from people, a relationship is a two-way street and it wasn't all on me.

"When I was little," I explain. "I was a painfully shy child. I found it difficult to hold conversations with my parents much less strangers. My parents took me to a psychiatrist at some point to see what was wrong and he diagnosed me with –"

"Social anxiety disorder?" he asks.

I smile. "Sometimes I forget you're a doctor."

"Can't turn it off. Sorry."

"Don't be. Anyway, he said I would grow out of it. When it came time for me to start school, the other kids noticed my quiet behavior and pegged me as someone to stay away from. So I got used to it and didn't reach out. I...I don't know what it means to have a friend. I only know what it looks like on screen."

He clears his throat and I think he's about to say something but he doesn't. I glance at him and can see that his eyes are more teary than usual.

"It's okay," I reassure him. "I'm used to it. People don't see me."

"That's not true," he says. "I see you."

For the next three hours, my mind replays memory after memory on the plane, at customs, and in the taxi. I see nothing and hear no one, no one but him. Our memories haunt me like a long lost friend. The first time we met, the jokes we shared during the clinical trials, the way he helped me when my parents were killed, his insistence on joining me when we were at the shelter. I think of our road trip to San Diego, the way he surprised me at Disneyland, how he got me out of federal custody. The first time he told me he loved me.

I sigh as the charter plane lifts off the ground. Norris and Eva become tiny specs in the distance below. Jason smiles and I know he feels the same relief.

"We made it," he tells me. I don't respond and when he looks at me, he can see tears welling in my eyes.

"What?" he asks.

"You came back for me," I whisper.

"I told you I would."

"Jason." I try to explain. "People don't come back for me."

"I do." he answers firmly. "I see you, Nicolette."

I look up at his sincere, cobalt blue eyes and all my frustration spills over.

"What's happening here?" I blurt out.

He looks surprised, almost flustered. And since I've already put it out there, I decide to just go for it.

"I like you," I admit.

"That's all you feel?"

I look down at my hands, feeling exposed. And defensive.

"What's it to you? You obviously don't feel the same," I snap.

"You're right. I don't feel the same."

His words knock the wind out of me. If he was going to hurt me, he could have done it more gently.

"I don't feel the same way because I don't just 'like' you," he explains. "I love you."

My heart just folds. Tears threaten to spill over and everything I want to tell him, everything I feel, I tell him through my eyes. He nods slightly, accepting everything I have to say and reciprocating the same. Once again we lean closer to each other as if our very eyes are magnets.

And in some random charter plane, flying over some random part of the world: we kiss —

—The woman yanks Jason to his feet. She sneers at me while she kicks him towards the edge. The gun fires.

"Ahh!" he cries out.

He topples over into the water below.

"No!" I scream, helpless. "Jason!"

BEEP! My eyes snap open, heart pounding. I look around, disoriented for a moment.

"Sorry," the man apologizes in Russian. I meet his eyes through the rear view mirror and stiffly nod. The man drives on and within ten minutes, we arrive at my destination. It looks just like it did in the picture Jason and I saw online. I quickly pay the man, grab my backpack and enter the building.

Twenty minutes later, I'm situated in the fully furnished one bedroom apartment.

The place has a cold, almost sterile feel to it. The furniture is dark and depressing and the gray kitchen counter tops add to the sullen mood. It's perfect. Jason and I figured we could brighten up if we had to use it but now that I'm here without him, I can't think of a better decor.

For the next hour, I sit on the kitchen stool and stare into space. Seeing but not really seeing anything. It's still light out. Russia is an hour and a half behind Sri Lanka. I don't know what prompts me but I finally stand and walk to the TV. Pick up the remote and turn it on. Immediately, the news, Russia Today, comes on. To my surprise, it's in English. I'm glad because my basic Russian would have only picked up a third of the information shared.

Sure enough, aerial images of the bridge appear on screen. Jason's picture and my picture are captioned along the screen. In bold, the headline reads: **"DR. JASON MONROE, TALLOWAY ACCOMPLICE, KILLED IN SRI LANKA. BODY FOUND IN RIVER."**

Shock ripples through me at the words on the screen. They found him. They found his body. To my surprise, something that I thought had already died dies once and for all.

Hope.

Hope that he had somehow survived. Hope that because I didn't see his body, he might have made it.

He's really gone.

The reporter, a young blond woman, says, "According to local authorities, Monroe was attempting to flee with Talloway when he was shot and held hostage by an unknown woman. She reportedly shot and pushed him over the bridge and into the river before Talloway broke loose and tried to save him. Several pedestrians reported seeing a woman who fits Talloway's description, emerge from the water and escape the pursuit. But Monroe never re-emerged. Three hours after the incident,

Sri Lankan authorities searched the river. They have confirmed the recovery of the twenty-two-year-old's body. U.S. officials have requested to have the body released to them."

I feel a burning sensation in the pit of my stomach at those words. They took him away from me. Now they want to take his body? *I* should be the one burying him. *I* should have that chance to say goodbye. I get so caught up in the rush of emotions, I almost miss the next words out of the reporter's mouth.

"Sri Lankan officials have already refused to release the body to the United States, pending further investigation into the circumstances surrounding the doctor's death."

I feel relief. The situation is out of my hands but I'm glad his body won't be turned over so easily. Jason loved Sri Lanka. I don't think he would have minded being buried there.

Jason's Wakefield Hospital portrait appears on screen and the guilt stabs me in the chest all over again. His life had been so uncomplicated, so promising before I entered the picture. I can't help but think I was the worst thing that ever happened to him. The thought is too painful. I reach over to turn the TV off but pause at the sight of the White House spokesperson on screen. He's a thirty-something-year-old man with thinning brown hair.

"President Lewis has personally stated that it is not the U.S. agenda to engage Nicolette Talloway in any sort of manhunt. We are currently working with Sri Lankan authorities to learn the truth about Dr. Jason Monroe's death. We are hesitant to point fingers at this time but question if the illegal status of the pair had anything to do with the incident."

I can't believe my ears. I listen harder to see if this man is really implying what I think he is.

"We are aware that Talloway and Monroe could not have gained citizenship at this time because the dual citizenship process has been temporarily frozen in Sri Lanka. It is unclear on which grounds they entered and remained in the country. Our hope is that it is not what ultimately cost Jason Monroe his life."

They're serious. They are actually pinning his death on the Sri Lankan government. It was carefully worded but the veiled accusation is bound to worsen relations between the U.S. and Sri Lanka. Wasn't there anyone with a phone recording the incident? Didn't anyone tell the reporters that the agents pursuing us were *white* with American accents? Or did the U.S. somehow suppress the public from disclosing that? I then remember the woman yelling in *Sinhala* before we got to the bridge. She spoke it fluently. Maybe people did confuse her with Sri Lankan authorities.

My head hurts. I shut off the TV and think on what to do next. Jason would tell us to pray and I know deep inside I should. But I don't know what to say. The last petition I gave was to find my husband and now he's dead. The dangerous thought creeps into my head. *God, how could you let him die? Why did you let this happen to him?*

I close my eyes and see Jason falling off the bridge, the blood red river below…

Call Eva.

I'm too tired to question it. To wonder if it's my thought or His voice. I walk to my bag, pull out my untraceable satellite phone. She answers after two rings.

"Where are you?"

CIA Headquarters - Langley, Virginia

Noelle

How did this happen? He wasn't supposed to die. I gave them explicit orders to bring them *both* in alive. The more I think about it, the more furious I get. Jason is dead. They haven't released his body yet but his body was found. The target is missing and her accomplice is dead.

But he wasn't just an accomplice. Tears threaten to spill over but I push them back, along with the memories.

I've never had a mission fail so badly - and so publicly. Obviously, the public has no idea of my involvement but that's because the higher ups had to step in and point the finger at the Sri Lankan government. I haven't seen Lewis since the meeting in his office but I'm sure he isn't thrilled about the worsened relationship with another country. I pace the length of my office. It's time to re-group. We're losing time and giving

Talloway more and more of it to get away. The first step to re-grouping is figuring out what happened.

A knock on my door.

I stride over to it, open it and nod at Bauer. I don't see the gentle giant in his eyes but I also don't see an ogre. I'll take it. We walk side by side to a nondescript room. I use my card and gain clearance. We walk in and find Agent Elena Marlianna seated. Security stands at the corner. I can handle myself but the woman is extremely lethal.

We take seats opposite her. Bauer pulls out her file, glances at me, and nods.

I take the lead. "What happened?"

Her dark blue eyes give nothing away. They're almost the same shade as Jason's eyes but he never had such a coldness in his. Now he's gone. She must read the anger in my eyes because she starts talking.

"Serafia and I found them on the beach. Monroe spotted us and alerted Talloway. We chased them across town. They were prepared and very aggressive."

"We warned you about their training," I remind her.

She nods. "They were even more experienced than a year ago. We walked in on Talloway finishing a Krav Maga class. She had a black patch on her arm."

If what she says is true, Nicolette Talloway is now an even match for any agent in our repertoire. I keep my thoughts to myself and hold my gaze steady.

"Why did you kill him?" Bauer suddenly asks. Elena's brows shoot up at his frankness. He's never been one to ease into a conversation.

She takes a deep breath and runs a hand through her short black hair. It falls back around her face perfectly.

"Self-defense."

I frown. She continues.

"Talloway was a formidable opponent in hand-to-hand but Monroe was the good shot. He tried to kill us several times."

"If he was a good shot, then why didn't he kill one of you?" I immediately ask. I don't believe her story for a second.

"He's a good shot, but we're better."

I hold the woman's eyes for several moments but neither of us gives. Bauer looks between the two of us, clears his throat, and tosses the file down in front of him.

"You're suspended pending further investigation into the veracity of your claims. Whether you re-join this case or start again on another, consider this a warning. My staff and I are not accustomed to covering up the mess field agents make."

She blinks at the swift decision and straightens in her chair. Her eyes dart between the two of us, as though testing to see if she can appeal.

"What of Serafia?" she asks.

"Malcolm Serafia has been reassigned to administrative work indefinitely."

Elena frowns in surprise.

I answer her unspoken question. "You are one of the agency's most brilliant assets. It's why we selected you for this mission. Once the investigation is concluded, you'll be cleared for work again."

"How long should that take?"

"However long it does take," Bauer replies and stands. The meeting is over.

We leave the room and walk several feet down the hall.

"You don't believe her," Bauer states. I nod. "Neither do I. Get back on the horse without her. It may be a good thing that she's fallen off."

He hands me her file and walks on.

"I can't help you anymore." Those are the first words that come out of my mouth the minute she answers.

Her voice is aggravated. "I thought the CIA wouldn't touch this with a ten-foot pole. What changed?"

"A lot of things," I hiss into the untraceable phone. "I'm too involved now. They could trace this back to me."

"You killed Jason." It's not a question.

I sigh. "It was never my intention for him to die. You know that. My goal was to apprehend them. The agent says she was acting in self-defense."

"Who?"

"You know I can't tell you."

"You hid the new plan from me. You didn't even allow me to warn them."

"I had to. The prey has become the predator."

"In more ways than one. Goodbye, Noelle."

10:00 AM - Next Day - Moscow, Russia

Nicolette:

I open the door and see the first familiar face I've seen in over a year.

Eva Bond.

She's still as beautiful as ever. Tall, thin, young, and dressed in all black as usual. The only thing that's changed is her hair. No longer is it a small afro but it has grown into a rather large one, now pulled back into a ponytail. She's packed light, with nothing more than a duffel bag.

"Hey," she says. She lets herself in, closes the door and immediately pulls me into a hug. My tears free fall. When she lets go, I see that her own eyes are moist. It's almost bizarre to have this moment, considering her history with Jason but it feels good to finally be with someone who knows he is worth crying for.

We walk over to the living room and sit in companionable silence for a few moments.

Finally, she speaks. "Tell me what happened."

I don't know how long it takes me to recount everything but somewhere along the way, my tears dry and a coldness sweeps over me as I recall the events that led to his death. By the time I finish, Eva is frowning hard, processing it all.

"The agent's name is Elena Marlianna. She's one of the best in the agency."

Elena Marlianna.

It feels weird putting a name to that face. The face of the woman who killed Jason. I much prefer her to remain a nameless psycho bitch.

"How did they find us?" I ask, toying with the throw on the couch. "We were off the grid."

"No, you weren't."

My eyes snap up to hers. She briefly closes them before facing my frown again.

"You never were," she continues. "The CIA knew the entire time. Deputy Director Edward Bauer wanted Carter out. He had no interest in you until Lewis did."

"And you *knew* this?" I feel anger surge through my chest. "You sent us to Sri Lanka knowing the whole time that they were on to us? You let us stay there even after we *asked* you?"

"Nikki, when I sent you, I didn't think he'd develop an interest and if he did, I thought I could get you out in time. When Jason called, there was still no indication that his stance had changed. It appeared the same as it had for over a year. I'm sorry. I had no idea they would do this."

"Jason is dead." I slice her with the words.

"Jason is with the Lord."

My eyes widen in surprise. I stand up and walk to the window. I don't know what to do with myself. I want to open the window and jump out. I want to turn around and wring Eva's neck. I'm angry and well trained enough that I could kill her this time. I want to lay all of the blame on her. If she had warned us ahead of time, if she had told us when we called, maybe we could have...

I know her apology is sincere and I know we were both at fault but it's easier to blame her. I feel stronger doing it. I want to tell her to screw herself and get the hell out of my apartment.

Clear as day, something Jason once said hits me and I know it isn't a coincidence. I can almost *hear* his voice.

"Forgiveness almost never starts with a feeling. It's a decision."

I take a deep breath and contemplate his words. I can feel her eyes on my back, waiting. I try to think of all the ways she helped us before. How she didn't have to do anything she did. How she risked her own life to set me free not so long ago. My anger starts to evaporate.

Then it dawns on me. Her hands were tied.

"The documents you gave us. The IDs and clearance and visas and permits." I turn from the window slowly.

"Your connection was in the CIA." It's more of a statement than a question. I'm almost certain by the time I voice it. I meet her eyes and see the confirmation there.

"They had to keep tabs on us in order to help you. You cut a deal with them."

"It was the only way," she replies.

"Who?"

"I can't say."

I frown.

"Whoever it is has betrayed us. Betrayed you."

She shakes her head. "The agenda has changed. It's out of their hands now."

I don't even try to decipher what she's said. I swipe at my eyes and turn back to the window. Eva stands and joins me there. It's unspoken but we both know the air is cleared.

We're good.

"They're after me," I say. "What do they want now?"

"I don't know. Let's find out."

And for the next three hours, that's exactly what we do. Research and try to find out what the CIA could possibly want with me. Eva explains that she confronted her contact and parted ways. That's when I understand. Not only is her contact distancing themselves for fear of being compromised and discovered, her contact is now in the center of the team searching for me.

Eva starts with a simple Google search. As soon as she types in my name, a slew of articles appear in Russian. Eva switches the language to English and we read. Most of them still have Jason's picture front and center with headlines about his death. We split the task and read them all. At first, it kills me to see the news of his death repeatedly mentioned but I eventually shut down and operate robotically, filtering the information I already know and making note of anything new. I know Eva can see the change. I feel her eyes wander to me more than once in the course of our research.

After another hour, we reach a breakthrough.

"Hmm," Eva murmurs. I look over at her. She beckons to me and points at her screen. It's an article that appears to have been taken down. The title is still fresh in the search engine: "Talloway's Blood: Secret Files of the FDA's Intentions."

"Look at the times." Eva points on the screen. It was posted at 9:00 AM in London and taken down at 9:16 the same morning. She voices my conclusion.

"If it wasn't legit, the U.S. government wouldn't have yanked it. Do you know how many stupid conspiracy theories they ignore on a regular basis? This story has credence."

I watch her track back to the blog the article was originally posted on, she pulls up the owner's bio.

Micah Jenner.

He's a biracial kid who can't be more than twenty-years-old, the founder and head writer of the investigative blog called *Veritas America*, based in the U.K. There are several other articles on me. Various articles speculate the true nature of my relationship with Jason. Eva finds his number. She picks up her phone.

"What if he doesn't know anything?" I ask.

"What if he does?" she counters.

Right before my eyes, her voice changes into a crisp British accent with a girlish lilt.

"Micah Jenner? Hi there, my name is Sarah Kind. I know about the hidden article. I have the link you need."

She glances at me. She makes an appointment for the next day. Promises to comp him if the lead is useless. I frown at the conversation. He seems a little naive and very inexperienced. He has no idea if her lead is legitimate and yet he agrees to fly all the way out to Russia from the U.K. at his own expense to hear what Eva has to say. No professional in their right mind would do that. Most wouldn't be able to afford it.

When Eva hangs up, she looks me over once more.

"You haven't slept." It's not a question. I'm not going to try to B.S. her. I haven't slept once since stepping foot in this apartment. I nod in confirmation.

"I can't."

"Try."

I walk to the bedroom and sit on the edge of the bed. I lie down and immediately start to drift. Whatever my mind was reluctant to do, my exhausted body is now more than willing. In the land between consciousness and slumber, it occurs to me that this is the first time in nearly two months that I'm going to bed without Jason by my side. I realize then it is one of the reasons I was so reluctant to sleep in the first place. It's just another event that cements him being gone.

CIA Headquarters - Langley, Virginia

Noelle:

The lead has gone cold. I pace the situation room as technicians and analysts sort through the data we have on Talloway. The situation room houses twenty computers, with a large screen at the center. I watch the technicians and analysts run around like chickens with their heads cut off, trying to pull something new out of a bunch of old data.

There's only one way to trace her now.

"All right, listen up!" I announce over the crowd. They fall silent. "New lead, new clue."

I hear the door open to my left and glance at it. I do a double take. The room quiets and my heart pounds as the last person I expect to see enters my domain. Elliot Lee. I frown. What the hell is he doing here?

He looks around the room and lifts a hand in greeting before meeting my eyes.

"Agent Jackson," he nods. "Excuse my interruption. By all means, continue."

He perches himself at the edge of a work station, in the corner, closest to the door he came through. My team turns back to me, expectantly. While I appreciate their ability to remain professional in the presence of a dignitary, I'm reluctant to proceed but have no choice. I mask my surprise, irritation, and worry - and continue in my confident facade.

"I want you to search for data under the name and passport of a 'Jennifer Dawson.'"

They search without question or hesitation. Immediately, a series of passport numbers appear on the screen, along with various countries. The number, burned into my mind, instantly stands out. I bide my time, though, and let them peruse through eight different passports before reaching it on their own.

859926439.

Up pops her picture. The technicians and analysts around me gasp. Like a dog that's seen its first meal in weeks, the men and women around me type at light speed and immediately pinpoint the passport's last location of use.

Moscow, Russia.

"Pull up the surveillance," I command.

We're immediately pulled to the Domodedovo International Airport. The flurry of voices drowns out my pounding heart. In a sea of Europeans, finding this girl is like looking for a needle in a haystack.

"Focus on customs." I remind them, "The passport claims to be from the U.S. Pull up surveillance from there."

All the screens turn to that section of the airport. I feel Lee's eyes on the back of my head as I walk through the desks, my own eyes fixed on the various screens. I'm moving on to the next desk when something stands out at the corner of my eye on a technician's screen.

"Hold on," I tell him. I point to the image. "There."

He zooms in, enhances it, and places the find on the big screen. It's her. Nearly indecipherable but I recognize the cap. It once belonged to Jason.

"She's definitely in Moscow," I say to no one in particular. "Run a search of all the hotels, apartments, any hostel that might be housing her under that name."

They get right to it.

"Agent Jackson." I nearly jump at the man's proximity to me. I turn to find him right behind me. "May I have word?"

"Got it!" a tech exclaims. "She's renting an apartment in the Zamoskvorechiye District."

I turn to an assistant. "Inform Bauer of the lead and request immediate relocation to Moscow."

I turn back to an expectant Lee. We leave the room and I escort him to my office. Close the door.

We face each other by my desk chairs. I don't offer him a seat and he doesn't ask.

"What can I do for you, Mr. Vice President?" I barely manage to keep my annoyance out of my voice. He may be good-looking and one of the most powerful men in the country but I do not like to be shadowed. He picks up on my irritation.

"I apologize for dropping in like that. I actually wanted to ask you a few questions but what I witnessed just answered them."

I say nothing in response and wait.

"Has President Lewis told you *why* he wants you to pursue Talloway?"

"Has he told you?" I retort, knowing the answer. His face flushes red and I'm surprised to see that he's capable of being embarrassed.

He shakes his head bitterly and says, "We both know I'm just a prop."

He's right. Lewis didn't like Lee and wouldn't have normally chosen him to be his running mate but he needed someone who added youth and charm to his ticket. He needed to shirk off the image of being a stodgy old president who would bring the same political corruption of past administrations. Lee, a passionate, handsome, and very young rising politician - was the perfect choice. If it weren't for Lee, Lewis probably would have lost.

But that doesn't give him an "in." Short of state dinners, and large affairs that require both of their presence, Lewis and Lee do not mix company. Lewis hasn't even given him reign to make diplomatic appearances like most vice presidents of the past.

Again, I remain silent.

"Does it bother you at all that he's telling the country one thing and commanding you to do another?"

He stares me down but still, I don't buckle. Of course I don't like it. But whatever his issue with Lewis, it has nothing to do with my job.

"How did you know about the Jennifer Dawson lead? No one here knew about a fake passport."

"What does it matter how I knew? It helped us get closer, didn't it?"

"Well, yeah…until she gets ahead again."

I narrow my eyes at him. His head is tipped in a show of curiosity, light blue eyes guessing far more than I'm comfortable with. It doesn't help that the quizzical frown on his face both irritates and arouses me. He needs to leave. I need him to leave.

"Did you still have something you wanted to ask me, Mr. Vice President?"

"Would you answer honestly, Agent Jackson?"

He knows. An entire organization full of the most brilliant minds in government intelligence and *he* is the one who sees the connection. Not just a pretty face after all. The question hangs in the air. So does the tension that comes with it. He looks down at me in full suspicion but something else flashes in his eyes. They shift again and flicker to my mouth and I suck in air in reaction. He feels it too.

Yeah, he needs to leave. *Now.*

"I'm doing my job, Mr. Vice President."

"Call me Elliot."

"No, I don't think I will." His dark eyebrows shoot up in surprise. Has it been that long since someone's denied him? "As I said, I'm doing my job. If you find something wrong with it or think me to be incompetent-"

"That's just it," he interrupts. "You're *too* competent. If something's going on - if you are compromised in any way and let's be frank, I think you are - then you are far too competent for others to find out. I'm not so concerned about national security as I am about your motives and what it is you really are hiding."

My stomach drops at his frankness. I feel a mixture of fear and something else as he steps closer to me. I can smell his intoxicating cologne. He barely leaves a breath's space between us when he finally looks down at me and says, "I'll probably find out eventually. But even if I don't...be careful, Noelle."

A strange thrill shimmies up my spine at the sound of my given name on his tongue. His eyes burn into me as he slowly steps away, turns on his heel and exits my office. I know he won't leave it alone.

What I don't know is why part of me doesn't want him to.

CHAPTER FOUR

Nicolette:

Everything is surreal. I wake up the next morning with stiff limbs. I glance at the clock, which reads 8:00 AM. So much for jet lag. As I get ready for the day, I'm grateful for the brief reprieve sleep brought. I thought I would be tortured by nightmares of Jason in my sleep. Instead, they were sweet dreams. Sweet memories. This is the second time I'm reminded of Jason's words on forgiveness and I wonder if God's trying to tell me something. I've been so consumed with running and figuring things out, that I haven't even decided what I feel *about* God at this point - not since I thought those accusatory thoughts. I can't make sense of losing my husband five weeks after we married. I can't make sense of such a blatant lack of protection.

And yet I know Jason is in heaven. I know his soul still exists and he's in paradise. I have no doubt about an afterlife. It's *this* life that screws with my mind.

What's heaven like, Jason? And when can I join you?

I miss him.

I can't do this anymore. I need to shut down, otherwise I'm never going to get out of this apartment and face the world. I want justice and an explanation. I want there to be recompense. I want them to pay for what they did to Jason. Not only for his death but the *way* in which he died. He suffered. The thought of it burns my stomach and fills my chest with a new surge of anger, one I am not going to let go of. I need the anger. I need it to move forward and not be crippled by grief. I enter the same mode I was in when I packed up my things at our house. A cold, robotic person replaces Nicolette and I walk into the living room, more focused than ever.

Eva is waiting, coffee in hand.

She looks me over and hands me a cup. "How'd you sleep?"

"Fine," I reply. I sit opposite her on the bar stool. She slides three passports across the table to me.

I flip them open; they each have my photo, with different names. One is from the U.S., one Canada, the other - Russia. I don't mince words.

"Can I still use these?"

Eva grimaces. "My contact didn't know about these ones. I had an extra set made just in case."

"When?"

"Last year. I made some for Jason too…" her voice trails off as she realizes the potential effect of her words.

I don't react. I bundle up the passports and stick them in my backpack. Inside are my clothes, my money, and the guns I never bothered to unpack. Something in me tells me to keep everything intact, so I do. We eat the takeout Eva ordered and leave for Taganskaya.

In the cab, I pull on Jason's cap and tuck my hair under its edges. Ten minutes later, we arrive at a nondescript café in the middle of the financial district. I wait near the entrance as Eva makes her way in and greets the U.K. blogger. He's about my height with a medium, muscular build, psychedelic hazel eyes and a buzz cut. Sharply dressed in a pair of khakis and a dark gray sweater, he's a handsome young man. I can see it all clearly. The surprise at "Sarah Kind's" real voice, her real name and the link that she has to offer. She beckons to me and I step forward.

His eyes widen as I approach the table, as if I were a fantasy come to life.

Eva watches in amusement as I sit across from him. After a couple of moments, he pulls himself together and extends a hand. I quickly shake it, cut to the chase, and skip the formalities.

"I'll answer your questions if you answer mine."

Just when I think he's a bit slow, he jumps right in.

"What do you want to know?"

"Who exactly is after me?"

"The President, the FDA, and they're using the CIA to do it."

"What does the FDA want?" I ask.

"I'm not sure."

I wait for him to explain.

"I know they want to secure you to harvest your blood but they have their own distribution scheme for it. It's different than the one proposed to you when your blood first became known."

"But you don't know exactly what that scheme is?"

"No. My source wouldn't allow me to read the file."

"What file?" Eva asks.

Jenner answers but keeps his eyes on me. "There's a file on the FDA's plan and distribution scheme for your blood. It contains a list of agreements between countries that have negotiated for first rights to the cure."

"What about the donations I've given?" I ask. Jason and I thought that by donating, the bidding war would end.

"Ah, the donations." Jenner leans back in his seat and shakes his head. "The file also reveals that a large portion of the samples you donated were apprehended before reaching their intended destinations."

"What?"

He nods. "They were stolen by U.S. intelligence black ops and given to international contacts in order to produce favors for the U.S. Domestic spies literally stole from St. Jude's and other nations to create a diplomatic auction. Why do you think the price of oil has recently dipped in the States? The U.S. struck a deal with Saudi Arabia. Twenty percent of our debt to China has been forgiven. It's no coincidence. If President Lewis can get his hands on the source - you - he can get the rest of the debt expunged."

I'm not surprised. It's the same thing Carter told me when she was in office. Offers have been flooding the White House since the day Jason and his team announced what my blood could do. Right now, it boils at the thought of countless children being denied the cure to cancer because their greedy government wanted a slash on oil prices and national debt. Little by little, my hope for humanity dims. So does my concern for it.

"How did you get a hold of this source?" I ask.

He shifts in his seat and looks around. "*Veritas America* is an upstart blog. My Dad helped me quite a bit but it's starting to bring in revenue. The bigger the story, the better chance we have of paying everything back and being in the green. Your story has been our biggest revenue-generator so I didn't think twice about meeting their price."

Eva frowns. "Checkbook journalism?"

He shifts in his seat again, this time defensive. "I had no choice. He is the perfect source and took a huge risk in telling me. If caught, he can never work with his organization again."

This kid is so green. If caught, the guy will be lucky to sit in a jail cell for the rest of his life instead of being killed.

"They took the article down."

"I know. Because I'm out of their jurisdiction, they were unable to detain me, despite several requests to the embassy. I managed to get off with a warning," he says with an almost smug expression. His expression shifts to one of desperation when he looks at me. "That's why I need your story. They can't take down this big of a lead, not when it comes directly from you."

I feel sorry for him. He's a rich kid, playing around with Daddy's money and he's in over his head. But he is trying to make a name for himself. He is trying to tell the truth. And he did give me a lot of information I can use.

"What do you want to know?"

He pulls out a recorder and looks at me questioningly. I nod and he hits the record button.

"Tell me about you and Jason."

So I do. I tell him everything from the time I ran to his house the night my parents died to the day of our wedding to the day he died. I tell him the truth about Jason's death - that it was U.S. intelligence that pursued us - Sri Lanka was our safe haven until then. I tell him the truth about our relationship and what he meant to me. For some reason, it's important to me that people know he wasn't just a rogue doctor-turned-accomplice. He was my husband.

"He was far more to me than anyone could ever imagine."

Those are the last words I say before Jenner clicks the device off. He finishes taking some notes before looking up at me.

His hazel eyes glow with sincerity when he says, "Thank you, Nicolette. I know that was hard for you."

It was. But I'm not about to cry any more.

"Who is your source?" I ask point-blank. He frowns.

"You know I can't tell you that."

"You can hint it."

He raises an eyebrow and looks between Eva and me.

He leans forward and whispers. "You already know him."

What? That's news to me. I wait for him to expound.

"You've known him since this whole thing kicked off. He sat at your parent's dining room table two years ago."

And I immediately know. Oh my God.

We leave the café a few minutes later and hail a cab. Jenner stays behind, already typing up the story. We decide to close up the apartment, cancel the lease, and grab Eva's things. On the ride back, the facts toss and turn in my mind like a salad in a bowl. I realize now that everything Jason and I thought to be true while in Sri Lanka was a lie. We built a perfect life for ourselves while everyone else lied and schemed around us. I zone out at the thought but thankfully Eva is aware.

The cab pulls into our street and Eva immediately tells the heavy-set driver, "Keep going. Don't stop."

I look up in time to see Russian authorities surrounding the building that was once my apartment. Though silent, siren lights flash on the tops of the cars and people, authorities, residents, and passersby flood the entrance of the building. I slowly lower in my seat as we pass the traffic and see several men and women dressed in similar suits. Though not dressed in distinct uniforms, I know they are of the same outfit: the CIA.

I turn to Eva beside me on my left and she's already on her phone.

"What are you doing?" I ask.

"Hacking," she replies. "Okay, he's in Paris. He checked into *La Tremoille* this morning at nine their time."

"What's the time difference?" I ask.

"Two hours behind."

I nod and turn to the driver. "Domodedovo Airport."

Eva shakes her head and tells him. "Sheremetyevo, please."

He nods his bald head and drives on while she explains in a low tone. "If they're here, they know you came in at Domodedovo."

"Won't there be security at all of them?" I point out.

"Yes, but they can only put so much man power in one place. They'll do it where they know you've been before."

Noelle:

The building is surrounded and they are nowhere in sight. Once again we've missed them.

Shit.

I stand in the middle of the cold, sterile living room and direct my team. There are about twenty of us crammed in the tiny space. Several analysts work in mobile stations, others search throughout the apartment; three assets stand on guard.

"Search for leads. Anything that might tell us her next step."

An agent finds a duffel bag and looks through it with gloved hands. My heart drops. I know who it belongs to. I had hoped against hope that she would stay out of this but she's here and she's made a rookie mistake that surprises even me. But as we sort through the bag, I realize that Eva wasn't that naive after all. The only things left in the bag are her clothes and a couple of rifles. No I.D., no passport, no documents.

Unless…

I stride over to the analyst's station. She's a newbie with small square glasses and a short brown bob.

"What's your name?" I ask unceremoniously.

She nearly jumps out of her skin at my unexpected attention. "Uh, M-Mi-Minka Beemer, ma'am."

"If I give you an IP address, can you pull up the user's deleted history?"

The analyst visibly swallows her nerves.

"I - I should be able to, ma'am."

"Then do it." I give her the number.

A voice calls to me across the room. "Agent Jackson, you might want to see this."

I walk over to his station and look over his shoulder at his screen. It's an asset's frequency. It appears as a tiny dot on the map of Moscow. Initially, I frown. We have at least thirty assets surrounding train stations, airports, and public transit stops around Moscow but then I see the name.

Elena Marlianna

Suspended until further notice but her frequency is on screen - and it's not her phone chip that our computer's picked up, but the tiny GPS chip implanted in her Achilles heel. The girl smartly turned off her phone, or is using another, but completely forgot about our other means of tracking assets.

"Follow her," I order the analyst. He assigns an asset to track her. Within minutes, their dots collide on the map. She continues her course and he follows close behind, unseen.

"Tell him to turn on his camera." The analyst sends the command to his phone. A few moments later, his surveillance of her appears on screen. It's not HD, but we can clearly see the back of Elena's head in a black taxi. She's appears to be trailing another vehicle and hasn't yet noticed the asset trailing her on his bike.

"Find out who she's following," I relay through the analyst.

The asset shifts his position to capture the car in front of her. Two heads appear in the rear passenger seats and I already recognize one of them. The rest of the room catches up when Nicolette Talloway turns her head in Eva's direction. They've studied her face long enough to recognize her profile.

Bingo.

I point to the three assets with me, take out my gun, and pull the slide.

"Let's go."

Nicolette:

Eva explains that the Sheremetyevo International Airport is on the northern end of Moscow and is the largest airport in the country. We plan to split when we arrive there, break off at different terminals and meet each other in the middle, barring agent interference. Our hope is that the size of the mammoth airport will work in our favor. Eva should be able to detect the majority of the agents once we meet up again. Until then, I'm on my own.

After we finish planning, the drive is silent for the most part. I glance outside and watch the numerous faces pass by. Once again, everything feels surreal. I would do anything to switch places with one of the people walking on the sidewalk. I notice a young couple pushing a stroller. The mother stops pushing as the father bends down to release the baby from her seat. There's no mistaking her gender with all that pink. He holds the kid, readjusting her on his shoulder and a thought stabs me in the chest.

That could have been us. That could have been Jason and I, give or take a few years.

The car drives on, too fast for the couple to stay in my line of sight. I crane my neck to get one last look at them when something catches the corner of my eye. Short black hair, pale white face, dark black shades. I would recognize that face anywhere. It's been branded in my memory since the day Jason died. Elena Marlianna. In the back of the car right behind us. I slowly turn back to the front and catch the driver looking at me through the rear view mirror. I look at Eva but she's already spotted the car.

"Can you shake them?"

The man nods and turns his eyes back to the road. Something rises in my stomach that I can't quite put my finger on it until I do.

Suspicion.

I feel uneasy and try to mentally calm myself down. If Eva is relaxed about it, still flipping through her phone, why am I a nervous wreck all of a sudden? The driver turns off of the main road and takes several short turns through alleys and side streets. I look back. Just when I think we've lost them, the car re-appears.

To my surprise, we pull up to a deserted church building. It's large and historic with one proud steeple in the center. Something's wrong. We're no longer en route to the airport, the driver pulls up on the wrong side of the curb, his vehicle opposing the flow of traffic, and he pulls the car to a complete stop on curb. Seconds later, the car following us pulls up.

I should have trusted my instinct. All of the glances, the suspicious tension, the convenient trailing.

This is an ambush. And we're the prey.

I glance at Eva and her face has hardened into stone. I slide my hand into my coat pocket and pull on the slide of the gun. The driver, predictable by now, pulls out his gun and points it directly at Eva's pretty face.

"Wait here," he says in a thick accent. "Or I will be forced to shoot."

Eva glances at me but remains still.

"Remember what I taught you that day?"

"I do," I reply. "But I have a cleaner way."

She raises an eyebrow as the driver looks between the two of us, sweat beading at his brow.

"By all means," she says calmly. "*Show me*."

That's all the cue I need. In an instant, Eva re-directs the vortex of the gun - she grabs his arm - shifts it to the center of the back seat while yanking her head to the left. He pulls the trigger and jerks his arm but the bullet merely shatters the rear window. I shoot through the pocket and hit him at the perfect angle. He slumps over, his hand goes slack.

Done.

Eva opens his door from the back and I attempt to push his body out. He's too heavy. We hear a car door closing behind us. Elena has gotten out of the car.

"Come on!" Eva yells.

Change of plans. I throw the backpack on, pull out my gun and exit the vehicle, facing the back. Eva leaves on her side and it breaks into chaos. Elena shoots at Eva while we both shoot at her. Using the car doors as shields, neither of us gets a hit. I glance at the church and make my decision.

For better or worse, I run to the building while Eva covers. I shoot at the window and jump through. I tumble in like a gymnast and, as I suspected, land neatly on the entrance floor. I'm lucky nothing was there but a soft church foyer. I pop back up and aim my gun through the window. I find my target and shoot. Elena ducks back behind the car door as I aim from a better vantage point. I manage to hit the car once. Eva uses the cover and joins me in the building. The minute she's in, we turn and run for it.

We race into the sanctuary, down the aisle, past the pews and up to the altar. On each side of the stage are short, winding staircases that lead to the second floor seating. I dash ahead and run up the right set of stairs.

Sun filters through the large balcony window, which would look serene if I didn't break it. But I do. I shatter the window with the butt of the gun and climb through. I'm on the roof. It's eerily quiet outside and the sun gives a ray or two of warmth in the brisk air of the day. I scale the roof with careful, quick steps, using my hands to keep me rooted. I move to the back of the building. Thank God for modern renovations on a historic building. A pipeline runs down the back corner of the church and I race towards it.

Shots fire as I rappel down the piping and I look up to see Eva shooting on the roof. The steeple blocks my view but I know Elena is on the other side.

"Eva, come on!" I yell.

"Go!" she yells over her shoulder. "I'll catch up."

I continue my descent down the pipe. By the time I reach the ground, my arms are on fire. Going back to the front is out of the question but there has to be an escape through the back. I look around and search for an out. There's a walkway leading from the back entrance of the church into the grounds. The grounds of the church are fairly traditional. The cemetery sits at the left of the walkway. A small maze sits at the right. Four yards beyond it, behind a wall of shrubbery is what appears to be an overpass girded by a wrought iron gate. I run towards the shrubbery when I suddenly hear:

"Warner, Kline, there she is!"

I whip around and see a man in dark clothing emerge from the side of the church, gun in hand. He's looking past me and I see two men emerge from the cemetery to my left. I dash into the maze and hear them run in behind me. I take several turns in the winding vegetation and tell myself to just move forward. If this is a simple maze, and it should be, given the size, then there's only one entrance and one exit. I stop at the edge of another turn, keep my gun extended, and listen. I can hear heavy feet running on my left, though the source of it is completely blocked by the high beams of hedges. He has no choice but to meet me here. So I wait. Moments later, he emerges from the turn I took. I shoot.

And miss.

The guy shoots back but I dodge it.

That's when he bum-rushes me. I kick straight at his groin and it slows his momentum but it doesn't incapacitate him like I expected. He continues to barrel forward and I toss the backpack to the side. Time slows down but our movements speed up. I see a flurry of forearms and fists and focus on blocking them one at a time. When I see an opening I take it with fist, my elbow, my foot…whatever will do the job. He tires. I can see the surprise in his eyes. He wasn't expecting me to be this good. I bury my foot into the side of his knee and hear a clean pop. He falls to the ground in time for his nose to meet the upswing of my knee. This time, it knocks him out.

One down, two to go.

I pick up my backpack and secure it over my shoulders. Stand at the edge of the turn and listen as his partner runs to our location. To my surprise, the footsteps overlap and I realize that the two are together! I pick up my gun and toss it back down. The slide is locked open and I can see it's out of rounds. I reach past him and pick up his gun. It's a standard Glock 26 and should do the job. The slide is already pulled.

They round the corner and I move fast. Drive the butt of the gun into the first guy's face. It connects with his eye and knocks him off his feet. Turn the gun on the other, hold my hand steady, and shoot.

This time, I hit. He falls and I flee.

I race towards the exit and within seconds, emerge from the other end. I find the gate door and cross over.

Eva is there, surveying the area. Her hands are empty, which tells me her gun ran out of rounds too.

She gives me a quick look-over, nods and starts running across the overpass.

"Going somewhere?"

We freeze and look back. Suddenly, a figure emerges from the shadows of the overpass entrance we just came through, gun pointed. The figure emerges into the full light and I gasp, reeling back. She's young, tall, thin, and black. Clearly an agent but one in authority from the looks of her tailored gray suit. None of this throws me off. It is the face that is the exact replica of Eva Bond standing next to me. Not even the most trained cosmetic surgeon could pull this off. It is a design strictly made by God while in the womb. The only thing that differentiates them is their hair. Eva's is an afro, this woman has hers straightened down her back.

She pulls a walkie talkie from her hip and speaks into it, gun still raised. "Code 104. I'm on the overpass behind the church."

"Noelle," Eva says in a wry tone, smile quirking the corner of her mouth. "Longtime no see, sis."

"Let her go, Eva." Noelle pleads, her voice both soft and authoritative. "Bring this to an end."

"You knew it would come to this."

"I hoped it wouldn't."

They stare each other down. I look between the two. Noelle finally shakes her head and peers at her mirror image.

"Why are you doing this?"

"You know why," Eva retorts.

"You and Jason had a fling eight years ago. Now all of a sudden, you have to avenge him?"

"He was a brother to me. To *us*! How could you let him die?"

"You know that was out of my hands."

Wait. She had something to do with Jason's death? Then it clicks. The suit, the way she carries herself. The fact that she wasn't with the other men but showed up later. She's leading the chase. She's in charge of the mission. I point my gun at her and see her straighten.

We eye each other but don't say a word.

I feel Eva stiffen beside me.

"I won't hurt you because of Eva. But if you keep us from leaving, I can't make any promises."

"Nicolette, I have to take you in."

"You didn't have to kill my husband, but you did it anyway."

"Husband?" Noelle frowns in confusion before shock stretches her eyes. She's speechless. And what can she say? She probably still would have ordered his hit even if she knew we were married.

"Noelle," Eva gets her attention once more. "We each made a choice several years ago. Mine was wrong in the beginning but now I'm making it right. Yours was right in the beginning but now it's going wrong."

"Eva, please." Noelle says, closing her eyes wearily. "We've already gone through this."

"No, we haven't." Eva says, her voice growing urgent. "I don't have much time, Noelle. Remember what Mom used to tell us. About God and all that?"

I glance at Eva and frown in confusion.

Noelle frowns in disbelief. "What does God have to do with anything that's going on here?"

"He has everything to do with it. Jason tried to explain it to me years ago but I didn't understand. Now I do. I used to be afraid of death. I used to be afraid because of everything I've done. But I'm not afraid anymore. I'm free. And you can be too."

I turn to Eva, now concerned. Her manner of speaking is off, like she's trying to say goodbye. She's backing towards the edge of the overpass, her back facing the railing.

"Eva," I ask. "What are you doing?"

She doesn't answer but reaches into her pocket and tosses me something. It's her phone.

"Yeah, what are you talking about?" Noelle adds, caught up in the strange conversation.

The glance she throws above our heads is so brief, I almost miss it. I turn around and follow her line of sight. To my horror, Elena is there, with a sniper rifle pointed directly at Eva.

"Ask Him, Noelle," Eva says. "Because my time is up."

I turn back in time to see Eva wink at me in unspoken assurance.

"Eva, no!" I scream. But I'm too late.

Her head suddenly yanks back, propelled by the force of the bullet. Her body topples over the edge of the overpass and into the busy street below. Several cars screech and horns blare at the sudden fall.

"Eva!" Noelle screeches. She runs to the edge of the rail and peers down for sight of her sister. I don't look with her. I don't want to see it. I don't want to remember her that way.

I use the opening and look for an out. It drives right under me. A ton truck with an open wooden cab is passing on the opposite flow of traffic. There's no time for fear. No time for calculation. I climb the railing——

"Hey!" Noelle yells from behind.

——and jump.

CHAPTER FIVE

Noelle:

It happens too fast. One minute, we're on the bridge arguing in a standoff. The next thing I know, Eva is dead and Nicolette jumps over the overpass. She lands perfectly in the speeding ton truck and drives out of sight. I can't think clearly. I can only see red as my mind jumps from target point to target point. I look up and see the next target moving.

The sniper. Elena.

I shoot. She runs. I don't know how much of it is grief and how much of it is desperation - the need to get *something good* out of this miserable situation. A large part of it is rage - rage at the death of my sister, by the very hand I just suspended. I run back through the overpass entrance, through the gate and past the church grounds. I see the edge of her jacket pass the corner of the church and shoot. The bullet clips the building but misses her. By the time I reach the front of the church, I'm panting heavily. I reach it in time to see the back of a cab turn the street corner, her black hair peeking through the back.

She's gone.

An armada of vehicles show up moments later but it's too late. My team assesses the damage. Three injured assets, one heavily bleeding from a bullet wound and a dead body whose face is identical to mine.

I'm reeling as we drive back to the apartment. My sister is dead. I hadn't seen her in five years. Never did I think the first reunion would be our last. We left so much unsaid. And now she's gone. I reach into my back pocket and pull out the wallet. I reach past my Virginia driver's license and feel the edge of a well-worn photo. I tug it out and feel a burning in my chest at the image. Two little girls in braided pigtails and red velvet dresses, posing in front of a Christmas tree. I'm on the left, with a shy, timid smile. She stands on the right, with sassy, confident eyes that speak of mischief. I can't remember if she'd had her fill for the day. There was always new trouble for her to get in.

Trouble. Trouble is what got her killed. A cold, numbing sensation fills my chest as I realize that my very last family member has died. Our family was never large to begin with. But I'm the last one standing.

When we arrive, I exit the car on autopilot. Those with me in the car took one look at my face and knew to shut up. It looks like someone gave them the memo at the apartment building. My team stares at me as I enter the lobby with heavy feet. They whisper and glance but keep silent when I pass and ride up the elevator. I appreciate it until I actually step into the apartment. The last person I want to see stands there.

"Agent Jackson," Lee nods in that authoritative way of his. He looks me over and frowns at the look in my eyes.

"What happened?" he asks.

I'm done.

"I'm sorry, but did the role of a vice president somehow change in the past two-hundred years to now include extensive involvement in CIA affairs?"

The team gasps around me and Lee raises an eyebrow on his otherwise indiscernible face but I continue.

"Why are you here? Why are you *always* here?" My voice is rising and his patience is shortening. He strides over to me, firmly grabs my arm and walks me into the only bedroom in that apartment. He shuts the door and the inquisitive eyes behind it.

He turns to me, his tall frame towering over mine.

"*Enough*. Tell me everything now."

"Why-"

"It's not just your career that's on the line!" he yells, his gravelly voice thunderous. "If the administration that *I am a part of* has anything to do with something unsavory, I want to know *now*. I arrive in Moscow thirty minutes ago and hear reports that someone fitting your description is dead; that Talloway escaped again, and you started chasing another agent like a mad woman. Then you show up, looking like death. You have ten seconds to tell me the truth or face the consequences when I get to the bottom of it myself!"

I break. The images rush back at me. Talloway's jump, Eva's assassination, the conversation on the bridge, the weight of what I've been hiding. And now, the glint in his angry blue eyes as he threatens the future of everything I've worked so hard for. My hands shoot up to my face and I fall back against the bed, folding forward as I do something I haven't done since my mother died ten years ago.

I cry.

The tears flow uncontrollably and so do the sobs. I can only imagine what I look like to this man but I'm past caring at this point. The weight is too much, the burden too heavy. I'm failing in every arena of my life and I've just lost one of the most important people in it. The sight of Eva toppling over, the sight of her body on the street, like a fallen carcass. The only person who has known me since birth is gone and I took her for granted while she was alive.

I've never felt so alone.

Suddenly, to my shock, I feel two strong arms wrap around me in a solid embrace. I bury my face into his shoulder and inhale his fresh cologne. His warmth is comforting, so is the feel of his hand stroking my back up and down. He probably does it just to calm me down but the unexpected gesture of comfort only makes me shake harder, cry fiercer. He waits, allowing me to wring out all of my tears, even as it ruins his suit.

Eventually, the shaking subsides and the tears come to a halt. He still holds me for a few moments longer. Finally, he reaches into his suit pocket and passes me a freshly pressed handkerchief. I dry my eyes and wipe my nose as he sits beside me on the bed. He's waiting.

"The body the team is referring to was that of Eva Bond, formerly known as Natalie Jackson, my twin sister."

I can feel his body stiffen in surprise but he thankfully remains silent. I continue.

"We joined the CIA eight years ago, shortly after graduating college. We both had basic training but I decided to go the administrative route while she chose to do black ops. She was one of, if not *the* best asset this agency has ever seen. Quick, cold, effective, and deadly. But she always had a penchant for trouble - even as a kid. Five years ago, she left the grid, changed her identity after completing a mission and dropped off the CIA's radar. They still have an investigative file on her but it went cold after two months."

"You knew?" he asks. I nod and he doesn't ask anything else.

"She was my sister. I wasn't about to rat her out. I couldn't keep consistent track of her because disappearing was what she did best. But she could always find me and managed to keep in touch."

He saves me the trouble of confessing and puts two and two together.

"She asked you for the passport and you helped her get it, didn't you?"

I nod.

"How did you do it without being detected?"

"I paid an upstart intern to make whatever we needed."

"And you didn't think it would be a big deal because the CIA had no interest in finding her at the time."

I nod again. "Bauer hated Carter. Wanted nothing to do with chasing Talloway. I almost thought he'd be happy at the thought of my helping her escape but I wasn't *that* crazy. I paid the intern, got it done, and asked very few questions. Just how Eva liked it."

I tell him how I sent my men ahead of me today but they were unable to detain them. I tell him about confronting them on the bridge, the way she died, how Talloway escaped. The only things I leave out are the last words we exchanged. He nods quietly, deep in thought. I stare straight ahead but can feel it when his eyes shift to my profile. He waits until I meet them.

"You could go to jail for this."

My eyes tear up again but I swallow them down. "I know."

"Why did you tell me?" he asks, his eyes intent.

I look at him, too tired to decipher him. "I don't know."

We hold each other's eyes for long moments, both of us silent. I enjoy my last moment of peace, fully expecting to walk out in cuffs.

Someone knocks. We both turn to the door. Lee gets up, walks over and opens it.

It's Bauer.

Nicolette:

My left shoulder is sore. I'm worried that I've broken a bone or wrenched a socket in the landing. I need to get out of here. Shortly after my insane jump, the truck exits the freeway and pulls into a busy shopping center. As he drives through an outside parking lot, I climb out of the cab, hang off the end of the truck and jump off. It drives on. I get strange glances from strangers but by some miracle, the driver doesn't detect me.

My shoulder is on fire now and my whole arm feels numb. Something is wrong. I rush into what looks like a convenience store and immediately catch the attention of the employees there. They don't say anything but they look at me strangely, not in recognition but concern at my pained expression and the way I'm gripping my arm. I probably look disheveled too.

"First aid," I say in Russian. One of the reps points to aisle four. I stride to it, pull the first kit I find, tuck it under my right arm and quickly slam more than enough money on the counter top with my right hand. I turn to the bathroom at the back of the store before the attendants can even speak. The minute I close the door, I strip off my backpack, jacket, and shirt. First things first. I place a firm hand on my left shoulder, take a deep breath and wrench it back into place. The pain is blinding and the shock of it knocks the breath out of me. My gasps fill the bathroom. Whatever relief I feel in having my shoulder back in place is suspended when I look at it in the mirror. Immediately, I see another problem.

There is something implanted in my shoulder and dried blood has streaked from the entry site. I push and prod at it and then realize – it's a *bullet.* The agent I fought in the maze. I didn't dodge his shot after all. I've never seen this before and feel like the subject of a strange sci-fi show. The dried streak of blood around my wound indicates that I bled but only briefly. The wound is closed around the bullet. My skin stitched itself back together over a wound that would ordinarily require stitches at the least. But I can't leave it like that. Even if I don't get an infection from the foreign object, the feel of it there is incredibly uncomfortable.

I have to get it out.

I wash my hands, open the kit, pull on gloves, and immediately go for the scalpel. I sterilize it then force myself to do what I would normally find nauseating. I swallow my fear and dig the edge of the blade into my skin. Ignoring the blood, I cut a small circle around the edge of the bullet, and dig into the new opening. I dig and push as blood streams past my shoulder and onto my chest. The tip of the blade makes contact with the bullet. I pry it out and hear it clink into the bowl of the sink. I check around the burrow of the wound for any shrapnel pieces. It's clear. Red but clear. I bite my lip and hold back a scream as I sterilize the wound with alcohol, pack it with gauze, and seal it with tape. I hope it will close on its own again. Otherwise, the stitching will have to wait.

I've got to get out of here.

I toss the contents of the rudimentary surgery away and clean myself up. My clothes are ruined with blood and I think that's what alarmed the employees the most. I change tops but wear the same jacket.

As I emerge from the bathroom, I can tell something is up. There are whispers in Russian. I walk down an aisle concealing myself from sight of the employees at the front desk. Through cans of shaving cream and deodorant, I see them. Three men in *politsiya* uniforms. I don't have time for this. I walk to the end of the aisle and make myself visible. The three men straighten and I see recognition flash in their eyes. One pulls his radio to his mouth. The other says, "Excuse me, ma'am," in Russian. I ignore him and turn into another aisle. I hear their feet scatter. I stride down one aisle and hear them stride down the one parallel to me on my left. I glance at the corner ceilings and, just as I expected, find large mirrors stationed on every corner of the building. I grab a can of what appears to be hair spray and pop off the cap. Stand at the end of the aisle and watch as one of the men bound down to my direction.

"Aminev," a *politsiya* suddenly yells in warning. He's seen the mirror and so does my target. Aminev reaches for his gun but I'm quicker. I knock his hand with the edge of my foot, strike the side of his head with my forearm and stomp my foot in my favorite place on the knee. He crumples to the ground and I quickly disarm him. I hold my hand steady and shoot out the mirrors. First one, then another, until all four are blown out. I barely hear the screams of customers as they race out of the building in a mad dash. I yank up Aminev by his uniform and plant the barrel of my gun into his dark hair.

His partners have no choice but to face me. Their guns drawn, they see they're at a disadvantage as their comrade lies in clear hostage. They come from separate corners but I can see them both. I look at the cop on my left and gesture to the cop on the right.

"Join him," I command in Russian. His eyebrows shoot up in surprise at my use of the language. He slowly moves to join the other officer.

I'm calling the shots now.

"Stand up," I hiss to the officer in my hands. He rises in pain and I can't help but think of Jason doing the same thing on the bridge. *Oh my God.* I'm doing exactly what Elena did to Jason.

Get it together, Nicolette.

I look at the other officers. "Lower your guns and kick them to me. Slowly."

They obey for the sake of their partner. I then order them to turn away from me and get on their knees, hands in the air. The minute they touch the floor I shove Aminev aside, rush to the two men and pistol whip them on the back of their skulls. I collect their guns then look around and find the back exit. More *politsiya* will show up in droves. I have to get out of here and fast.

At the back of the store, I toss their weapons into the dumpster and walk past several blocks of buildings before emerging through the front of the shopping center again. I look for the building I spotted while on the truck and find it. It has bright red lights and triple X's lined across the front. There's no doubting it's a sex shop but it just might have what I need. The owner there is much less concerned about my behavior than the employees in the convenience store. Maybe it's due to years of being discrete. She checks out my purchases with barely a blink and allows me to change into some of them in the dressing room.

Minutes later, I emerge from the shop in a platinum blond wig, dark pair of leather pants, and a pair of pitch black shades. My jacket is packed in my bag and in its place, I wear Jason's old sweater. I pull his cap over the wig and keep my head low. *Politsiya* cars surround the entrance of the convenience store eight blocks away and I keep my pace even for fear of drawing attention to me. I manage to hail a cab and drive past the chaos unseen.

Noelle:

Bauer walks in, uncertainty stamped on his normally confident face. His subordinate and his superior are in a bedroom in the middle of an operation and he doesn't know how to handle it. He looks between the two of us and focuses on me.

"Are you alright?" he asks in a surprisingly gentle tone. I look up and meet his eyes. The gentle giant is there. I nod and glance at Lee. Bauer turns to him.

"What's going on?" he asks, formalities aside.

"Agent Jackson just learned of some shocking news," Lee says. I look at him and frown. Why is he prolonging this? Does he expect me to rat myself out all over again?

"Natalie Jackson," Bauer says quietly. "They found her body on the E105 this morning. Said she was helping Talloway under the alias 'Eva Bond.' You know anything about this?"

I open my mouth to just spit it out and get it over with when Lee speaks.

"Of course she didn't. Can you imagine her shock when she confronted the two of them on the overpass?"

I look up at him in shock. He just covered for me. Stopped me from confessing.

"She told you what happened?" Bauer asks.

Lee nods and meets my eyes while he answers him. "Yeah, and I don't think she needs to repeat it."

Relief floods me at the sound of his words but so does confusion. He went through all this trouble to find the truth only to cover it up himself. Why is he doing this? Why would he protect me this way? I try to read it on his face but his eyes are as closed off as I've ever seen them. And yet, for some reason, I still feel safe.

I feel a hand on my shoulder and look up at Bauer's kind eyes once more.

"Are you sure you're alright?" he asks again.

I nod. This time I mean it. I know I'm supposed to act shocked and devastated. And in many ways, I still am. My sister is gone and Talloway is still on the run but Lee's just thrown me a lifeline. Rather than looking a gift horse in the mouth, I'll take it.

Moments later, we emerge from the bedroom, a trifecta of authority. My team must notice the difference in me because they finally start to approach me with their progress. Minka, though shy, beats the crowd and meets me first.

"Agent Jackson, here are the results of the search."

I scan through the articles and land on the pulled article title. The words immediately jump out to me.

"Bauer," I call him. He reads it and agrees with me. This is our next lead.

"Look up a blogger by the name of Micah Jenner," I announce.

Bauer passes the title to Lee. Lee frowns.

"'Talloway's Blood: Secret Files of the FDA's Intentions.' It wouldn't be pulled if there wasn't credence to it. Who is this Jenner?"

It's not about Jenner. I understand what they don't. The article was the only clue Eva needed to start her own investigation. She probably tracked Jenner down, asked him for his source, and was on her way with Nicolette to get to the source when she died. It's not about Jenner but whatever information he told them, we need to know. We're at least two hours behind their trail.

"New assignment. Find Micah Jenner."

"Micah Jenner is dead," an analyst replies. We all turn to him in shock. The room quiets down several notches. The three of us stride to his station and look over his shoulder at the report.

The headline reads: **"BRITISH INVESTIGATIVE BLOGGER, MICAH JENNER, SHOT DEAD IN FRONT OF SHEREMETYEVO AIRPORT."**

Bauer reads the article aloud. "According to several eye witnesses, Jenner fell to the ground in front of the international terminal with a shot to the head but the shooter was unidentified and unseen. Authorities have reason to believe the heinous act was done by a professional."

"Elena," I immediately say.

"He was the only one who knew about the file," Lee says.

"Assuming it exists," Bauer qualifies.

"I think it does," I say. Immediately my mind flashes to the folder I saw on Lewis's desk. I mention it.

"Do you remember?" I ask Bauer. He nods, though I can tell he doesn't want to.

An idea comes to mind. I gesture to Minka and she rushes over.

"Minka, I need you to pull up Elena's mainframe."

"Do you want a clean hack?" she asks bluntly. I nod.

Within seconds, the data appears. Elena's schedule, allowance, and most importantly - her assignments. On record, she is suspended, but in actuality, she's been given secret clearance.

"Who issued it?" I ask.

Minka pulls up the data. It's catalogued under a code I haven't seen before.

Bauer swears beside me. We look at him.

"Only one person has the authority to use that code."

Lee and I wait in rapt attention.

"Lewis."

Shock ripples through me.

"Why would he subvert the very operation he's assigned us to?" I hiss at Bauer, astonished.

Bauer shakes his head. "I don't know, but he's the only person who can use this code. He's the only person who has the password to do it. No one, not even the Vice President," Bauer glances at Lee, "can do it."

"Minka, pull up Elena's assignments."

It's a revelation. Her mission is dual in nature. Apprehend Nicolette alive and relatively unharmed but terminate all who stand in the way. One by one, her tasks lay out before us and it is a clean list that leaves a trail of bodies in its wake. Jason Monroe is the first name listed.

"He put a hit on him? *Why?*"

"You know why," Lee says. I look at him and he explains. "Jason always stood between the authorities and Talloway. And if left alive, he would have done everything in his power to get her out, legal or illegal. We all remember her break in San Diego. With him out of the way, you guys would have clean access to Talloway without any threat of him returning."

He's right - the logic makes sense - but it's the logic of a cold-hearted psychopath. And Elena is no better. I knew her story about Jason was bogus but I had no idea it was this sinister.

"Did you know they were married?" I ask them quietly. Lee looks at me sharply and Bauer's brows stitch down in surprise.

"When did that happen?" Lee asks.

"I don't know," I murmur, still picturing her on the overpass. "But she referred to him as her husband."

I can still see the anger in her hazel eyes. Her face was flushed as she spat out the words to me. Nicolette isn't just fighting for her freedom. She's fighting for justice. For Jason.

I shake myself out of it and re-focus on the task at hand.

Elena.

From our perspective, she's a double agent. Pretending to take orders from one authority when really taking orders from another. Jason, Eva, and Jenner are all listed and crossed off in order.

"What's her next target? Just Talloway?" I ask Minka.

She refreshes the page and a new name appears.

I gasp.

"From the FDA?" Lee asks.

"Jenner's source," Bauer concludes.

"Where is he now?" I ask.

The male analyst beside Minka pulls it up.

"Paris, France - checked in at *La Tremoille* this morning."

"She's two hours ahead. How are we gonna make it?" I ask.

"Air Force Two," Lee replies. His expression reads that he's dead serious. "Let's go."

CHAPTER SIX

Nicolette:

"Would you like anything to drink?" the flight attendant politely asks.

"Water, please." I reply, keeping my head averted.

She passes me, the last person on the aisle, a drink, and moves on to the next row. The exchange, though simple, is a nice reprieve from my manic thoughts. Thoughts that have been flooding me since I sat down in the plane. By some miracle, I managed to book and board the flight despite the heightened security at the airport. There were agents, none who recognized me in my blond get up, but oddly, there was also a fleet of *politsiya* roaming the airport and huddled around the front. Something happened at one of the terminals but I neither had the time nor the inclination to investigate. If anything, the incident provided a distraction for me to get through security faster.

But now that I'm not moving, my mind has time to wreak havoc.

Eva is dead.

Killed in an even more gruesome way than Jason was. Guilt once again simmers through me. Had I not called her, she would still be alive. She knew what she was getting into. Maybe more than I did. All the same, I've lost yet another person important to me. Next to Jason, no one has ever helped me the way she did. No one has ever stuck their neck out like that. She was the one who helped me transform. From a helpless teenager to a woman who can handle herself. She did that for me. Her confidence made me confident.

And yet, for some reason, I can't even cry. I sobbed and sobbed when Jason died. But when the friend closest to us both passes, all I can do is think about it clinically. Her death brings more questions than answers. Why didn't she tell me she had a twin sister? Was that her CIA contact? It had to be. How else would she have gotten such assistance? If Noelle is in charge, why would she allow her sister to die? And did she? She seemed just as shocked as I was when Elena pulled the trigger. Now that I think about it, the only one who saw it coming was Eva herself. I want to dwell on the tragedy that is her death but the questions keep me from doing so.

It dawns on me.

I'm becoming numb to death.

Not only did I lose her in a violent manner, I killed a man just minutes earlier than that. The cab driver's face is a blur in my mind. I don't know if he was married, had kids, a family that will miss him. And worse, I don't care. The minute he pointed that gun at Eva's face, it was game over. The same cold efficiency washed over me at the convenience store, when I held the *politsiya* hostage.

What have I become? I remember talking Jason through things after we first arrived in Sri Lanka. The amount of guilt for the various guards he injured or killed when breaking me out of the holding facility in San Diego. He prayed for weeks about it before finally accepting the forgiveness God was already offering. But I can't relate. I don't feel any guilt because it was all self-defense.

Wasn't it? A small part of me wonders how much of it was me doing what I had to do and how much of it was pure apathy, fueled by anger. There's an anger that can rage inside you and burn you up until you can no longer stand to be in your own skin. And then there's an anger that burns up every bit of feeling you have left. It fuels you but it also deadens the empathy, the mercy, the need to care. It's a dangerous sort of anger because you can do anything when you truly don't care anymore.

Now I'm worried. I'm not afraid of dying. I'm afraid of dying and never seeing Jason again. Can God accept me after the violence I've committed? Can He accept me even if I'm not sorry? And what is wrong with me that I don't even feel a little bit of regret for what I've done?

Forgiveness may be a decision but it's one I haven't made. And more heads will roll until Jason - and now Eva - gets the justice they deserve.

I stand up and enter the plane's lavatory. Inside, I peel off the edge of my shirt and examine my shoulder. I test the pain of the wound through the gauze and feel nothing this time. Carefully, I pull off the tape and peek under the gauze.

Nothing.

The wound is completely sealed and clean. The skin is stitched together so tightly, so smoothly, it looks as if nothing had happened. After more than two years of being aware of what my blood can do, I'm rarely ever surprised or awestruck by my body's mechanics. But this is one of those times. I remove the gauze and the tape and toss it in the trash.

When I return to my seat, I notice the overhead television. It's parked on an international news station and the headline reads: **"BRITISH INVESTIGATIVE BLOGGER, MICAH JENNER, SHOT DEAD IN FRONT OF SHEREMETYEVO AIRPORT."**

I freeze. Slowly sit down and process even more information. Footage shows the *politsiya* surrounding the front of the airport, the same place I passed when entering five hours ago. The screen then cuts to his picture. I can't hear anything because I don't have headphones plugged in to the jack. The man next to me notices me straining to understand what I'm seeing. He reaches into his briefcase and hands me a pair of earphones. I smile my gratitude and plug it in, catching the last half of the female reporter's sentence.

"Just prior to his death, Jenner released one last article, featuring an exclusive interview with Nicolette Talloway, the young woman whose blood can cure cancer and other illnesses."

The screen then cuts to another picture and I inhale sharply. A watershed of feeling rises up in me but I shove it back down again. I can't afford to lose it.

It's me. And Jason. In Sri Lanka on our wedding day. The photo I took with me the day he died. Jenner asked for permission to use it but I didn't think he'd get around to posting it so quickly and I didn't think I'd actually see it plastered on TV. He must have written the article the minute Eva and I left the café.

"According to a recording Talloway consented to, Dr. Jason Monroe was not only Talloway's accomplice in escaping U.S. authority, he was her husband. The two married in a private ceremony in Sri Lanka just weeks prior to his death. And Talloway provided even more shocking insight into the nature of Monroe's death."

My voice plays over our wedding photo. "Jason was not the casualty of a belligerent Sri Lankan police force. They had nothing to do with his death. The people who pursued us, the person who killed him - were American. It was the CIA."

The reporter comes back on screen. "White House spokesman, Alan Tremell, has yet to respond to Talloway's direct contradiction of his statement regarding the events surrounding Monroe's death."

What else is new?

The reporter then turns to a panel beside her and they begin to discuss the new revelation. They speculate over the U.S.'s true role in Jason's death and the motivations behind it. My hands start to shake when they talk about the two of us.

"In all this time," a male panelist says. "I never thought of Monroe and Talloway as a couple. For some reason, I just asexualized their relationship and dismissed it as friends on the run."

"Or even a mentor helping a kid out," a female panelist adds.

"Really?" a different one asks. "It's no surprise to me. They were only three years apart in age. He was twenty when they met and she was seventeen. They got to know each other really well during the research of her blood. And I think his decision to stand by her when her parents were killed speaks volumes of his intentions."

"I agree," the reporter cuts in. "I mean, let's be honest, there has been speculation about the true nature of their relationship for years and now the public finally knows the truth. Look at that photo."

It comes on screen again but this time I've girded my heart and the tears stay at bay.

A panelist's voice speaks over the image. "They really were a beautiful couple. And clearly very much in love."

I pull the headphones off and place them in the briefcase of the now-sleeping gentleman who lent them to me. I can't go down memory lane. Jenner's naive face flashes in my mind. I think of the security in front of the airport. Elena must have killed him shortly after getting Eva. Everyone around me is dropping like flies and I suspect the only reason I'm alive is because of my blood.

If he has any brain cells left in that head of his, he'll try to leave *La Tremoille* as soon as possible. The only thing that could possibly be holding him is the money Jenner told me he was wiring to him. I know that once that clears, he's out of there. I glance at my watch. The plane lands in ten minutes. Once I get off, I have no time to waste.

I think in lists again. Get off the plane, secure my checked-in backpack, loaded with carefully packed ammunition and the permits to carry it. I use my new passport to clear customs and quickly run to the bathroom. In there, I change clothes once more, toss out my blond wig, and replace it with a dark red one. On my way to the exit, I see a flower stand with an array of beautiful, bright bouquets. A plan formulates in my mind and I buy the largest one they have.

La Tremoille is a four-star hotel near the heart of Paris. I only have one shot to get to him and it has to be through the front desk. The minute I exit the taxi, I pull on Jason's cap, straightened my back, hold the flower arrangement close to my face, and enter the hotel.

"May I help you?" the female front desk attendant asks in a pleasant French accent. It never ceases to amaze me how many internationals speak English in their own country.

I address her confidently, "Spencer Graham's room, please."

The attendant takes one look at the effusive arrangement and looks up his data.

"Er, he is in room 423. If you like, we can have a bellhop deliver them for you."

"And take my tip?" I reply half-jokingly. "No, thank you."

The attendant laughs at my quip and points me to the elevators. Moments later, I emerge on the fourth floor and quickly follow the numbers down the odd side of the hall. I barely register the rich decorations. I see a trash can stationed in the center of the hall and move to toss the stupid arrangement, when I see him. Graham. Emerging from his room with his suitcase in tow. If this hotel really is as fancy at it looks, it will have a security guard on call with cameras monitoring the halls. I glance up from under my cap and, sure enough, there are two black orbs housing security cameras on the corners of the hall ceilings. I reach into my pocket and slowly pull out the gun. I quickly stride to the man, and just as he looks up, pull the slide of the gun with a discernible click, pointing it at him through the cover of the flowers.

"Going somewhere?"

Noelle:

We're on Air Force Two. When we were at the White House, I felt butterflies at being in such a place of importance. No such feelings bombard me this time around. We're all too occupied with tracking down Elena and stopping her in time.

My team remains seated in the area reporters typically occupy but Bauer and I are huddled with Lee in his flight office. Bauer pulls open his personal laptop and once again breaks through Elena's mainframe. He attempts to reverse Lewis's assignment but is immediately rejected by the system due to rank. Lee tries to use his own password but the system rejects him too.

When it takes us to the Elena's home screen, a new directive alarms us.

I read it aloud. "Apprehend Talloway by any means necessary, barring death."

"Oh my God," Lee whispers. "How could Lewis consent to that?"

"How could Lewis consent to those other hits?" Bauer points out.

"Okay," I say. "Our only option is to get to Graham first. Try to head her off."

"And if we don't?" Lee asks. "Listen, I hope we can stop her in time but if we don't, we lose the only person who can tell us what this file really contains."

"Can't you?" Bauer asks.

Lee frowns. "I don't follow."

"The file is in the FDA's jurisdiction, not ours. The FDA doesn't have nearly as much red tape as the CIA. Can't you access it?"

I nod, already hoping against hope that Bauer's wager is correct. Lee frowns in thought. He shakes his head.

"Even if that were true, I know nothing about the FDA's system or how to access their documents."

"We do," I quickly reply and pull Bauer's laptop to myself.

Within minutes, I switch from the CIA's database to that of the FDA's.

"Why do you have access to their stuff?" Lee asks and then shakes his head and smiles at me. "Forget I asked. You're the CIA."

I smile back and pull up the FDA file data. There's an entire folder dedicated to Talloway. I manage to access it on my clearance but can only open the files from years prior to this one. The most recent file, one entitled "Operation Windstrom," requires an executive-level password. I hand the laptop to Lee and he enters it.

Bingo.

Nicolette:

Spencer Graham.

It's only been a year and a half since I last saw him but he's aged since then. His gait is slower, less confident and there's gray peeking left and right in his dark, thinning hair. I force him back into the room behind the bouquet and kick the door shut behind me. The suite is mid-sized with a queen-sized bed and couch situated to the left of the door and a desk neatly situated to the right. He rolls his luggage to the side of the bed and I turn to throw the bouquet away. It's a test.

And he fails.

The minute I turn my back to him, he lunges for me. I block his arm, kick out his knee, and turn, connecting my elbow with his jaw. He stumbles back in surprise but lunges for me again. I use the heel of my palm to break his nose and this time he folds over the side of the bed. I shrug off my backpack and lay it on the desk nonchalantly. I open it and pull out the supplies I'll need. Paper, pen, a recorder, and some rope.

I see him lunge once more out of my peripheral view and lose patience. I turn to him, point my gun, aim towards the ground and shoot.

"Ahh!" he cries in excruciating pain as the bullet pierces his left foot. He bowls over and falls to the floor.

I lay the gun on the table, out of reach, grab him by the arms and pull him to a chair. He groans, whimpers and curses the whole time.

"Shut up or I won't help you," I say in a quiet voice. His noise immediately dies down with the exception of an involuntary whimper. I tie him to the chair and sit opposite him.

"Please don't kill me," he cries, sweat beading across his forehead. His breathing is labored and I know I'll have to help him soon before he loses too much blood.

"The quicker you answer my questions, the quicker I'll help you."

We don't have much time. The shot probably alerted the staff. I click the recorder on.

"What is your name?"

"Spencer Graham."

"Who do you work for?"

"The FDA."

"Did you leak information to Micah Jenner?"

He gasps and begins to perspire even harder.

"Relax," I assure him. "I'm not going to hurt you." I amend my sentence because I just did. "I'm not going to kill you. Just answer my questions. Did you leak information to Micah Jenner?"

He nods. "I did."

"What information is in the FDA file regarding Nicolette Talloway?"

He frowns and gives me a strange look, like he's trying to figure something out but he shrugs it off and answers, his pain loosening his tongue.

"It's a file that details the FDA's plans for distributing the blood once the source is secured."

"What is it called?"

"Operation Windstrom."

"Who authored it?"

"Commissioner Richter Shaw."

"With whose authorization?"

"President Bentley Lewis. Lewis is the one who commissioned the new operation."

"Where is the file?" I ask, clicking off the recorder.

His eyes drift to his satchel. I unzip it and pull out a plain manila folder, only decorated by the formal FDA emblem and a stamp that reads "Top Secret." I open the file and read.

Noelle:

Just when I think Lewis's depravity couldn't get any worse, it does. Bauer, Lee and I look through the files and can't even begin to fathom which part is more corrupt.

Lee reads a portion aloud. "Secure Nicolette Talloway in order to gain unlimited access to the curative blood. Systematically administer the cure to the entire nation."

The "system" is horrifying in and of itself: first politicians, then military personnel, then children, and finally adults from the upper 2% before trickling down to the bottom 98%. The file lists various prices for the blood, aggregated according to what economist estimate consumers would be able to afford at each socioeconomic level. The plan details agreements between insurance companies and pharmaceutical companies. It even makes reference to researching if the blood can be watered down or rendered less effective so that people can still have minor ailments that would require medication.

These people are sick.

Bauer looks it over once more and says, "It looks like they plan to get the majority of their revenue and rewards from international entities. Once every American receives a portion of her blood, they plan on selling shipments of it to international ties for economic and diplomatic incentives. Oil price reduction, debt forgiveness, increased trade…"

Lee points to the screen. "Look. There's a list of the nations they've already given *stolen* samples of the blood to. They intercepted Talloway's past donations and re-routed it for financial gain."

I shake my head. "I don't understand. Lewis can't get credit for this without looking like a slime ball. He even plans on doing this in public. Why would he risk his career like that?"

Bauer scrolls down the screen. "That's why."

I read the information and gasp. There's a stipulation in the agreement that requires the pharmaceuticals to give a cut of their revenue to Lewis for his re-election campaign. Based on their trajectory, he will have more than enough to drown out his competition, regardless of his corruption.

Suddenly, the screen closes out on us. Lee clicks on it and tries to log in again.

Access denied.

"They locked us out," Bauer says. He looks at Lee. "They detected you on it and revoked your access."

"Great," Lee says. "How are we going to expose him if we don't even have the evidence?"

He looks at me and shrugs. "Now what do we do?"

Nicolette:

One would think I'd be surprised by the plans laid out by my dear motherland but I'm not. I'm not surprised, upset or outraged. That requires too much energy. I'm simply pissed. And being pissed is all I need to expose Lewis for the corrupt P.O.S. slime ball he really is. I flip through the file once more, trying to see if I missed any other relevant information.

"Please," Graham rasps behind me. I turn to him and see that his suit jacket is drenched in sweat. "My foot…"

I put the file under the recorder, far out of his reach and go to him. I pull off his shoe and he cries out in pain. Next, I pull off the blood-soaked sock. To my surprise, it's a clean wound. The bullet went straight through. I peek in his shoe and see the bullet roll to the back of the heel. It's still messy, though. Blood oozes out of the flesh and refuses to coagulate. I go to the bathroom sink, wash my hands, grab a clean white hand towel and wet it as well. I clean the wound as best I can before reaching into my bag. I don't have a syringe but I do have a knife. I clean the edge before running it across the heel of my left palm. Blood immediately runs out and I drip it directly over his wound. He tries to yank his foot back.

"Hey! What the hell are you doing?" he says in shock. It then dawns on me that he doesn't recognize who I am in this wig. I roll my eyes and yank off the thing, letting my jet black hair fall down around my shoulders. His eyes widen in surprise. His mouth hangs ajar.

He looks back down at his foot and his mouth stretches wider still. I look down and frown in surprise as well. The wound has stopped bleeding and the edges of the skin are starting to seal right before our very eyes. I notice that my blood isn't dripping anymore. When I look at my palm, I see the reason why. The wound has closed completely. There's no scar, just the remnants of my dry streaked blood.

I look up to find Graham watching me. He's speechless. I'm glad. I take the knife and cut him loose. I reach down and put the wig back on, tucking my black hair back into the edges.

He watches me silently as I gather my belongings. The authorities are only minutes away from surrounding this room. I pick up the file and calmly shove it into my bag.

"Wait, you can't take that." Graham finally speaks.

I roll my eyes and point my gun. "Try to stop me and it'll be your other foot."

He immediately puts his hands up and backs several feet away. I stride to the door, confident that he won't follow.

"Wait, Nicolette." I hear him call behind me. I turn and meet his eyes, already halfway out the door.

"I'm really sorry about this," he says. His eyes are actually sincere. "About everything."

I want it to mean something but it doesn't.

So for his sake more than mine, I simply say, "Apology accepted," and leave.

CHAPTER SEVEN

Internet Café - Paris, France

Nicolette:

I move quickly and ignore those around me. The minute I reserve my computer, I monopolize the café's copy machine and make at least five copies of the file I've acquired. I scan the originals and email them to myself. The next part involves research. Had Jenner lived, I would have sent him the files immediately but now I have to think outside the box.

I pull up various American news outlets: CNN, MSNBC, Fox, the New York Times and others. I then look up some U.K. outlets: The Daily Mail, the Daily Mirror, BBC, etc. I copy their fax numbers before monopolizing the fax machine. In the middle of my fourth fax, the whispers of the employees pick up in volume. I glance at them in annoyance, only to find them staring at the overhead television. An employee turns it up.

Footage features *La Tremoille*, in real time, about thirty minutes after my departure. The news is in French but I can infer what has happened from the bold headline: "SPENCER GRAHAM - U.S. FDA - MORT" featured in the headline, his picture captioned on the screen, and the numerous police cars surrounding the entrance of the hotel. Natalia was always the expert in French but I know enough of it to know that Spencer Graham is dead. He never made it out of that hotel alive.

Suddenly, footage cuts to the hotel's hazy security footage. I recognize it immediately. It's the hallway to Graham's room. I see myself approaching him with the flowers. From the angle of the camera, it's impossible to see the gun I was holding through the bouquets. The footage then cuts to me exiting his room, minus the bouquets. I can't understand what they're saying. I wonder if they think I killed him and am glad I decided to trash the wig and switch hats the minute I left the hotel. My black hair fans around my face and my new cap shields my eyes. I keep my head low and continue to look at the screen. Just when I think I have to get out of here, new security footage pops up. It shows me entering the hall elevator to exit. Almost as soon as my door closes, the other one opens and out comes Elena in all black. She reaches into her pocket and brazenly pulls out her gun before aiming it at the security cameras and shooting them blank. I know she killed him shortly after.

The screen cuts to the reporters, a man and woman who shake their heads at the images.

The woman murmurs, *"Quelle chance pour la femme avec des cheveux rouge."*

I decipher it enough to know that she says I'm lucky. And I agree. I escaped the crazy bitch just seconds before she landed on the floor.

I feel a sense of urgency and I can't put my finger on it. While the rest of the café continues watching the news, I finish faxing the documents. I then go back to my computer and load the scanned files. What if the faxes don't go through? What if they cover up the story or yank it off like they did with Jenner?

I go to the one website I haven't visited in over two years and load the files. I pull out the recording chip and load the audio. The images come up as new photos and the audio appears as a video but I neglect to write a status. Within seconds, comments, likes, and shares flood my once-dead Facebook account.

I log out and close the browser.

It's out there. It's done.

A weight I didn't know was there finally lifts off my chest. I got the truth and I revealed it. Hopefully some heads will roll. I lean back in my chair.

And then sit up.

Something buzzes at the bottom of my backpack and I dig through it to find the source.

It's Eva's phone. I almost forgot that she tossed it to me right before her death. It takes me a few seconds to configure the screen but as soon as I do, Elena's image appears. I don't understand at first. A button appears beside her picture that simply reads "Assignments." I hit the button and gasp.

I understand now. Right before the ambush, Eva had managed to hack into Elena's phone from her own. She wasn't just casually flipping through it in the cab. Somehow, I'm seeing her live feed and every assignment she has. Graham's name is coded in as "complete." So is Eva's...

And Jason's.

I go back to the main screen and navigate to the assignments. There's only one marked "pending." I click on it and feel my stomach drop. Two pictures: side by side of a blond brother and sister with bright blue eyes.

My brother and sister - Natalia and Nathaniel.

I bolt up from my station, shove my belongings into my bag and book it to the street. I hail a cab and hand the driver the address.

"Dépêchez-vous, s'il vous plaît!" I ask him to hurry in an urgent tone. I don't need to tell him twice. His speeding and quick navigation puts New York cab drivers to shame. Right as he pulls up to Nate and Nat's apartment, I see her step in.

Noelle:

We stride across the tarmac to a group of cars.

"Graham is dead," an analyst informs us.

"Shit," Bauer mutters.

"Minka, who's next?" I ask. She taps several keys on her laptop with one hand, while managing to keep up with us. She gasps and turns the screen to us.

"Oh my God," I murmur.

Lee pulls out his phone and to my surprise, begins to speak in fluent French.

He hangs up and says, "We need to split. I have a meeting with President Sion. He's sending security there as we speak. Call Natalia and tell them to get out of there."

He climbs into a black, well-tinted car and it immediately pulls off. We quickly climb into our own car and it pulls off too. Bauer instructs the driver to floor it and tells him the Talloways' address.

"What's her number?" I pull out my phone. Minka recites it as I punch it in.

"Bonjour?" a cheerful, cultured voice answers. Her accent is so on point, I almost think I've dialed the wrong number.

"Is this Natalia Talloway?" I ask urgently.

A long pause.

"Who is this?" the voice is no longer cheerful and the American accent is back in full swing.

"This is Agent Noelle Jackson of the CIA. Natalia, listen to me. You and Nathaniel need to leave your apartment right now. President Sion has security personnel en route to meet you outside."

"Why? What's going - AHHH!" the sentence immediately cuts off into a scream.

"Natalia? Natalia can you hear me?" I yell into the phone. There's shuffling. The sound of a male voice.

"Nate, get down!" I hear her yell.

A shot fires off. The line goes dead.

"Natalia? Natalia!"

Nothing. We have to get there. *Now.*

Nicolette:

I lunge at her just as she kicks through the apartment door. Natalia screams as I body check Elena into a wall. Her arm lands across its surface and I use the resistance to knock the gun out of her hand.

"Nate, get down!"

An errant bullet goes off before the gun lands on the ground. Elena drives her knee into my torso - I fall back - swallow the pain in my gut. We circle each other, testing the limits. She strikes, I block. I strike, she blocks. We circle once more. She charges - I shrug off my bag and throw it at her head. Her hands go up instinctively - I use the opening and strike as hard as I can. The tip of my toe connects with her groin - she doubles over. I lunge again - she tosses the bag aside - blocks my arm - lands a fist into my cheek. I turn over. The pain rocks me for a moment - the living room briefly blurs. I hear her coming from behind. I kick but she grabs my right leg and pulls - I fall - she drags me across the floor on my stomach. My vision clears. I yank my leg back - propel her forward just enough to turn — connect my left heel to the side of her head. She reels back and loosens her grip. I jump up and charge. She strikes - this time I dodge the blow and grab her arm - pull her to me and wrap my hand across her face. I yank hard and hear a pop. She topples to the ground. She's still conscious.

But barely.

Tries to get back up but stumbles. I walk over to the gun, pick it up and aim it at her pretty face.

She looks up at me, defeat clear in her unfocused eyes.

"Please," she rasps out.

"You killed him," I bite out. "I surrendered and you still killed him."

"I didn't have a choice," she slurs. "I was ordered. Eva was my friend and I still had to do it. I didn't want to but I had to."

"Jason was my husband. Believe me, I want to do this."

"Nikki, don't." I look up and see Nathaniel's pleading eyes. I almost forgot they were in the room.

"Nikki, please. Jason wouldn't want you to do this."

Nate's words pierce my core. I glance at Natalia who is eyeing Elena scathingly then meet Nate's sincere blue eyes again.

"You didn't see how he died," I say quietly.

Nate nods. "I heard how it happened. I heard the interview you gave. What she did was atrocious. But what would you gain by killing her?"

"Justice," I reply.

"Vengeance is the Lord's," Nate gently replies. I blink in surprise. Nate's a Christian? *Since when?*

I shrug off the convicting words, Jason's words of forgiveness and turn back to Elena. Her eyes are clearer now, though still unsteady and I stiffen my arm holding the gun. I may be a bad shot but I definitely won't miss this time. Had I done this earlier, Jason would still be alive.

Natalia finally speaks up. "Nikki, I don't blame you for wanting to kill the bitch. But if you do, this would be murder. You'd be killing a human being."

"I've done it before," I say brusquely. I feel more than see them blink in surprise.

"Oh," is all Natalia can say.

"Please," Elena rasps again. "I don't want to die."

I frown at the words and something akin to rage floods my senses.

"And what about Graham? Jenner? Eva? Do you think they wanted to die? What about *Jason*?" I scream at her.

I'm done talking. I raise my other hand to the gun but right as I do, I hear several feet rush to the entrance of the apartment.

"Nicolette, don't!" Noelle yells. I re-direct the gun at her and the two men flanking her side draw their own guns. She gestures at them and they reluctantly lower their weapons.

"She's moving!" Natalia warns. We turn to see Elena sluggishly adjust her position. She bowls over on her side and vomits. Natalia's face contorts in disgust. Elena tries to stand but I immediately re-direct the gun at her. The men flanking Noelle's side also point at her. She glances up and puts her hand up in surrender.

"Nicolette," Noelle begins. "You don't want to do this."

"Yes, I do." I reply. "You don't understand."

"Don't I?" Noelle replies, irritation in her voice. "You saw what she did to my sister."

I remain silent, keeping the burning question to myself. Noelle looks at me and answers what I refuse to ask.

"Elena Marlianna was suspended two days ago pending investigation into the unauthorized death of Jason Monroe. I gave her explicit orders to bring you both in alive. Little did I know she had contradicting orders from someone else."

"Lewis," I say.

She nods, frowning at my knowledge of this.

"He not only ordered the hit on your husband but also my sister. Believe me, I want her dead too."

"Then by all means." I raise the gun a few inches at Elena and she stiffens once more.

"Nicolette, if you kill her now, you'll get a short term victory for a long term loss."

I wait for her to explain.

"We need witnesses," Noelle explains. Understanding immediately floods me. "Elena is the most valuable witness we have who can attest to Lewis's deplorable actions. If you kill her, you kill the one person who can ensure that *he* pays. If it wasn't for *him*, none of the people we loved would be dead."

Jason's face flashes before my eyes.

And with startling clarity, I realize that if I do this, I wouldn't be honoring Jason's memory. I wouldn't be honoring everything he taught me about life, God, treating others, and rising above one's pain. The practicality of keeping Elena alive no longer matters to me. But neither does my thirst for revenge. Because that's really what it was. Revenge - not justice. And the Jason I loved would say the exact same thing Nate just told me.

Vengeance is the Lord's.

Something in me wilts and I lower my gun. The men accompanying Noelle lift Elena to her feet and cuff her from behind. They begin to move her away.

"Wait," I say.

I can't explain what's happened. I've done everything I can to avenge Jason's death - to make other's pay for it. To somehow make it matter. But no matter what I've done in response, the truth remains the same. Jason is dead. This personal mission of mine is over. I've gotten what I *thought* I came for, managed to rise above my most animalistic instinct, and still feel empty.

There's only one way to honor Jason. There's only one thing I *know* he would want me to do. I approach Elena and see the apprehension on her face. I feel Noelle, Natalia, and Nate's eyes on me. I stare into the woman's deep blue eyes, almost the exact shade of blue Jason's eyes were.

"I forgive you."

I hear several gasps around me but I only see her eyes. They blink in surprise, almost disbelief; and for the smallest moment, they shift from a defensive coldness to a look akin to gratitude. Elena says nothing in response to my words. But I don't need her to. Her actions no longer have any power over me. I realize that I haven't just freed Elena from what she did to Jason.

I've freed myself.

And that takes all of the fight out of me. All of a sudden, the emptiness lifts.

I'm free.

I feel a strong arm wrap around my shoulders. I look up into my brother's kind blue eyes and they beam with pride at what I've done. That one look confirms that I made the right decision. So does the peace that overwhelms my soul. He folds me fully into his arms and hugs me so tightly, my ribs start to shift. I raise limp arms to hug him back then start to pull away. But he holds on longer. And longer.

By the time he pulls away, I see tears streak down his flushed cheeks. I frown.

He answers the question in my eyes. "It's been almost two years since I last saw you. I've missed you."

Before I can answer, Natalia enfolds me in her arms and my nostrils fill with the scent of her delicate, flowery perfume. Her soft blond hair tickles my cheek. I enjoy the little reunion for what it is.

I don't have Jason anymore. But I still have my family. I still have Nate and Nat.

I'll take it.

Under Noelle's orders, the men have escorted a sober, but well-restrained Elena out of the apartment into full U.S. custody. For a few minutes, it's just me, Noelle and my siblings. For the first time, I'm able to take in their plush surroundings. It's the complete opposite of how Jason and I lived in Sri Lanka. The apartment is fairly large with a clean, minimalistic look: white couches, black tables with sharp, clean edges, ample floor space. The walls are stark white, only adorned by a black and white painting. A tasteful vase graces the fireplace mantel. It's clean, sharp and borders on the edge of cold. Mom would have loved it. Natalia always did have our mother's flare for interior design.

None of us really say anything. I think Nat and Nate are still in shock over what went down. Noelle has a lot on her mind and so do I. I see her glance at me from time to time but I give her no assurance. This forgiveness thing is starting to annoy me. I feel the tug to forgive her but I resist it. She may not be as diabolical as Lewis but she did send Elena and the other agent after us, with no warning to Eva, who could have helped us stay ahead. When she looks my way for the umpteenth time, I finally meet her eyes and stare back.

What?

"Operation Windstrom," she says quietly. "Where is the file?"

"It's secure," I reply.

She sighs at my evasiveness and Natalia frowns at it. She looks between the two of us and frowns even deeper before turning to Noelle.

"Do you need the hard copy or something? Because the file is splashed all over the news." She lifts up her phone and shows it to her. Noelle straightens and checks her own phone. I do the same.

Sure enough, my Facebook posting and numerous faxes spread like wildfire.

Noelle frowns at her phone before looking up at me in confusion.

"Why didn't you say anything?"

"Why should I?" I retort. The truth is, I didn't know. Almost as soon as I made the file public, I was rushing to Nate and Natalia's aid. It hasn't crossed my mind since. But Noelle doesn't need to know that.

I don't owe her anything.

Nicolette.

She leans back at my sharp tone, understanding washing over her expression.

"Can I talk to you for a moment?"

I sink further into the couch, obstinate. "I'm tired."

Nicolette.

What is that voice? I must be more tired than I thought because clearly I'm getting delirious. Noelle looks at my siblings, eyes pleading for assistance. Nate nods and stands; so does Natalia.

"We'll give you two a moment."

What are we? A couple? They leave the apartment and step out into the hall. Noelle leans forward on her lap and meets my eyes.

"Okay, I'm not good at preambles so I'll just come out and say what I should have said earlier. I'm sorry."

Surprise ripples through my chest but I don't let it cross my face. She elaborates, her eyes sincere.

"I am so sorry for my involvement in this entire operation. The minute my supervisors recruited me to find you, I should have turned it down and continued helping you instead."

Her words confirm my earlier suspicions.

"So it was you," I murmur. "You were Eva's contact."

She nods. "Eva asked for assistance when Jason sought her out. It…was a risk but I decided to help."

"Why?" I ask. She's right. It was a huge risk and could not only have ended her career but landed her in jail. My anger thaws just slightly at the thought.

She shrugs. "For several reasons. Like Eva, I too grew up with Jason."

"He never mentioned you," I say.

"When I joined the CIA, I asked him and the shelter not to. Under any circumstances. Jason kept his promises."

I nod in agreement. Every promise he ever made to me, he kept. I understand his confidence in this matter but am once again amazed at the loyalty of the Harvest Hope Baptist Shelter family. They never betray their own. Ever.

Noelle, looking at her feet, continues. "Anyway, Jason was like a brother to me. I liked him, I loved Eva, and I knew it was the right thing to do. *That* compelled me more than anything else. I never could have predicted being assigned to track you down. Suddenly, what I was doing in secret was in opposition to what my job now required of me."

I believe her. I don't need her to explain anymore.

"I forgive you, Noelle."

Her head pops up in surprise. Jason's right. Forgiveness is a decision. Like a clog that's been removed from a pipe, the one last obstacle to me forgiving is removed and the ability to do it gushes forth once more. I look into her eyes and nod in confirmation.

"I accept your apology and forgive you for it all."

She frowns, not understanding. She knows I'm being serious but it's as though she's unable to fathom why she doesn't have to beg and plead for it like she expected. She opens her mouth to speak but I hold up a hand.

"Think about what your sister said today. The same reason she felt free is the same reason I was able to forgive Elena. The same reason I'm able to forgive you."

It's hard to believe that all of this happened today. But between gun fights, chases, international flights, and changing time zones, it's only mid-afternoon here. We're both silent for a few moments before Natalia and Nate re-emerge. They look between the two of us, sense that everything's okay, and get to work at setting the apartment straight. I know I should offer to help but I can't. I'm so tired. The adrenaline has abandoned my blood stream and left me exhausted.

Minutes later, more people show up and cramp the once-spacious apartment. I gather it's a mix of the CIA, French policemen, and high level French security. Noelle stands to face the armada. I don't know what she whispers to them but it's enough to have them keep a comfortable distance from me. The room falls quiet when two men enter the space with even more security personnel flanking them. The man on the left is young, rather handsome, with a blond buzz cut and piercing blue eyes. The man on the right is almost as young and just as handsome with jet black hair and charming green eyes.

I recognize them both. Vice President Elliot Lee and French President Antoine Sion. I stand.

My sister steps forward and smiles at the French politician, putting him at ease.

"Ah, Natalia!" he says pleasantly enough. He kisses her cheeks and nods at my brother in greeting. Natalia and Sion exchange a few words in rapid French. Sion introduces Natalia to Lee. I feel Nate step to my side and place a comforting arm around my shoulders once more. Natalia finally switches to English and turns back to us.

"Allow me," she says. "President Sion, this is my sister, Nicolette Talloway. Nikki, this is President Sion. He was kind enough to extend President Hollande's offer of political asylum to us."

I nod and eye the politician warily.

Sion extends his hand and pulls me into a half-embrace, kissing my cheeks.

"Mademoiselle Talloway, it is a pleasure. I hope you feel welcome in France."

Lee extends his hand after Sion releases me. "Nicolette, I'm-"

"I know who you are," I interrupt. I frown at his hand then meet his eyes. "You're a part of Lewis's administration."

I don't add anything else but the accusation is clear. Guilt by association. Lee shakes his head adamantly.

"Not anymore, I'm not. I was unaware of Lewis's actions until I assisted Agent Jackson and Deputy Director Bauer in uncovering his true intentions. I want to assure you that neither President Sion nor I support his behavior or his intentions. We're here to protect you."

"Qui," Sion agrees, nodding. He gestures to the minimalist furniture in the room. "May we sit?"

"Of course!" Natalia replies and makes a welcoming gesture to the furniture. Nate sits next to me on the love seat, making it impossible for anyone else to sit close to me. Something in his guarded expression tells me he did it on purpose. He briefly catches my eye and winks.

Vice President Lee starts. "Nicolette, I want to apologize to you for everything that has happened in the past few days."

"I thought you were unaware of Lewis's conduct?" I reply.

He nods. "I was. But that doesn't bar me from apologizing on behalf of the U.S. government. Thanks to your work, Lewis is exposed for the type of man he truly is. It's only a matter of days before they impeach him."

"Like they impeached Carter? Only to have her stay in office?"

Lee blinks at that but continues. "We're not here to force an extradition on you. You're a U.S. citizen, not a U.S. prisoner. I'm extending my protection to you."

I see Noelle frown out of the corner of my eye. She's curious. She's been a silent observer this entire time.

"If you choose to return to the United States, I will do everything in my power to ensure that you live there as a free citizen without any obligation to the government or general society. *If* you ever choose to give blood again, it will be of your own volition."

I'm not impressed.

"How are you able to make such promises?" I ask. "You're not the President right now. Who's to say I don't land and get carted off to another holding center until you can follow through?"

Lee nods expectantly. "You're right. This is why I met with President Sion prior to coming here. He has agreed to offer you political asylum here along with your siblings until things have settled on my end. Again, it's up to you if you want to take it."

Sion looks at him and nods before turning to me.

"Nicolette," he says in a cultured French accent. "You can ask your brother and sister. France has been very friendly and welcoming to them. I want to personally extend an invitation to you as well. Only..." He glances at Lee, who frowns at him in surprise. "My invitation to you is not temporary. Hollande agreed to allow Natalia and Nathaniel to stay in France indefinitely. My offer to you is the same."

Lee raises an eyebrow but keeps silent. Noelle's frown deepens at the politician's last minute amendment.

I open my mouth to respond but then hold my tongue. It's one thing to call the Vice President out on his magnanimous B.S.; it's another thing to jeopardize my siblings' situation by being a jerk to the man who has allowed them to live in his country.

President Sion's crystal green eyes peruse my face with keen perception.

"No blood required," is all he adds. My eyebrows shoot up in surprise. He read my thoughts.

I look between the two men - both have sincere expressions but I trust neither one. I glance at Natalia and her swift nod urges me to say yes. I glance at Nate and appreciate the poker face he puts up. He wants me to decide on my own. I make a practical decision and turn to Lee.

"I appreciate your offer," I reply. "But it will be snowing in hell before I ever step foot on U.S. soil again."

I turn to Sion, stand and extend my hand. "Thank you for the offer. I accept."

Sion's face breaks into a huge smile and he stands to shake my hand exuberantly. He quickly turns to his men and starts rattling off in French. Natalia nods in agreement and I infer that they are making arrangements for my stay. Nate gives me another hug then heads down the hall to prepare my room, a huge smile on his face. Now that I've decided, he allows me to see it's the choice he wanted me to make.

Noelle approaches me and extends a smooth brown hand. I immediately shake it.

"I hope you're happy here," she says. "You deserve it."

"Thanks."

Lee, though outdone, smiles calmly and stands to shake my hand as well.

"My offer is always open to you, Nicolette. Just remember that."

My eyes bore into his. "Actions speak louder than words, Mr. Vice President. Isn't that the saying?"

"What do you mean?" he asks point blank.

"Make them pay," I reply. "When there are no consequences, there is no accountability and a nation without accountability is a nation that can't be trusted."

CHAPTER EIGHT

Three Weeks Later - CIA Conference Room - Langley, Virginia

Noelle:

It's over. It's finally over.

There will probably be some final hearings here or there to tie up loose ends but as far as I'm concerned, the whole mess is over. I sit in the conference room, waiting for Bauer, and turn the volume up on the news. A brunette reporter speaks.

"The nation is still reeling in the aftermath of the Nicolette Talloway scandal. A story that would more likely fit the plot of a movie than the chambers of Congress. FDA Commissioner Richter Shaw was removed from office in a resounding unanimous vote. He has left without severance and his pension has been revoked. Former President Bentley Lewis managed to escape impeachment by resigning - the first president to do so since Richard Nixon in 1974. He still faces federal charges of murder, perjury, obstruction of justice and malfeasance, otherwise known as abuse of power, while in office. The public generally horrified by the revelation that the former president issued orders to former CIA agent, Elena Marlianna, that were contrary to the orders of her direct supervisor, Special Agent Noelle Jackson."

The station airs the security footage from *La Tremoille*, showing Elena exit the elevator and approach Graham's room, shooting out the cameras before she reached him.

"These orders resulted in the deaths of three U.S. citizens and British investigative blogger, Micah Jenner. Among the U.S. citizens killed: Talloway's own husband, Dr. Jason Monroe and FDA representative,

Spencer Graham. Former agent Elena Marlianna struck a plea deal with the Department of Justice, admitting her direct involvement in the victims' deaths while serving as a witness to testify against Lewis. In return for her testimony, Marlianna will face a reduced prison sentence of fifteen years without the chance of parole. She has also been banned from the CIA. Unless newly-sworn-in President Lee repeats history and grants Lewis a full pardon, Lewis could face more than one-hundred years of prison time."

I tilt my head to the right and peruse the screen. They make no mention of Eva. No mention of her involvement in the entire situation. They don't even mention her real name in the list of those who were killed by Elena. I think to the private burial I held for her. The only people present were the members of the Harvest Hope crew. In death, just as in life, Eva had things done on her terms: shrouded in mystery and veiled with mystique.

The screen cuts to footage of a haggard looking Lewis exiting a courthouse and walking to his car, surrounded by the press and shielded by security and a fleet of attorneys. It then cuts to the transcript of the last known recording of Spencer Graham, abbreviated for key data.

"What information is in the FDA file regarding Nicolette Talloway?"

A pause...then, "It's a file that details the FDA's plans for distributing the blood once the source is secured."

"What is it called?"

"Operation Windstrom."

"Who authored it?"

"Commissioner Richter Shaw."

"With whose authorization?"

"President Bentley Lewis. Lewis is the one who commissioned the new operation."

Not even those lawyers can get Lewis out of this mess. A pardon is his only hope.

One *I* hope he doesn't get.

I hear the door open behind me. I glance at Bauer, who walks in, eyes on the screen.

"It is still unclear as to how Talloway secured the file from the late Graham and managed to expose it across the Internet, including via her personal Facebook page. Though creatively choosing to use social media to expose Lewis and Shaw, Talloway herself has been anything but social during her recent adjustment to life in France."

The screen cuts to Nicolette in Paris. She's walking down a street surrounded by press. Security creates a buffer. I feel a slight twinge of regret for that. She's safe but her location is now known. And with that, her anonymity is a thing of the past.

"President Antoine Sion has been vocal about his support of the Talloway family, especially the latest member to accept his offer of political asylum. Talloway lives with her brother and sister in their Paris apartment and has yet to make a comment on the fallout surrounding the file she's exposed."

The reporter goes on to talk about the numerous people speculating over Talloway's intentions. Will she continue to donate blood or keep it all to herself? Is she under an unspoken obligation to do so or has the death of her husband negated any obligation she might have felt towards society?

I turn off the TV and give Bauer my full attention. He pulls out a chair and sits next to me at the conference table. His blue eyes assess mine for a minute or two before sliding a piece of paper across the table to me. I pick it up, look it over and feel my heart pound in my chest.

"What is this?" I ask.

"You know what it is," he calmly replies.

"How long have you known?"

"Since it started. I'll admit I didn't know where Natalie was. But the minute private shipments to an 'Eva Bond' surfaced, I put two and two together."

"Why didn't you say anything?" I ask, dumbfounded. "Why didn't you stop me-?"

"Why would I?" he replies. "I had no reason to when you first did it. And by the time Lewis called us in, you had ceased most communication."

"So that's why you chose me for it. Because I already had the connection."

He shakes his head. "I chose you because you are one of the best special agents this unit has ever seen. I chose you because I knew you would do the right thing and not take the easy way out."

I.e. killing everyone who got in the way of my securing Talloway.

I look at the paper again. It's simply a statement sheet verifying the complete disintegration of all traces to Assignment A5367 - the deeply buried, completely unlogged task I bribed an intern to perform when helping Eva. Bauer could have destroyed me with the discovery. Instead he destroyed the discovery for me.

"Lee protected you," Bauer says.

I meet his eyes again and nod slowly.

"He wouldn't do that for just anyone," he says, his eyes telling me he knows something I don't.

I frown at his words but refuse to ask what he means.

"Where do we go from here?" I ask instead.

Bauer stands and walks to the door. "You tell me."

My frown deepens as I follow him down the hallway. We turn several halls before he leads me to an empty office, this one with more privacy. My frown turns into a blink of surprise.

"President Lee."

Elliot Lee turns from observing the floor-to-ceiling library and gives me a generous smile. My stomach tightens at the sight. As usual, he looks as fine as ever, in a well-tailored navy suit. The light blue dress shirt brings out his eyes. I shake my head at myself. I sound like a schoolgirl.

Focus, Noelle.

"Agent Jackson," he says, sounding genuinely happy to see me. The light in his crystal blue eyes match the bright smile on his face. Is it because of me or is he just happy? I shirk the thought - he has a lot to be happy for. I glance at Bauer, who gestures at me to go in alone. I step inside the office but before Bauer closes the door, I stop him.

"Thank you, Ed." I say. "For everything."

The gentle giant flashes briefly in his eyes before he nods and says, "Let me know what you decide."

He closes the door. I frown once more at his words. What decision is he referring to?

I turn back to find Lee watching me, waiting. It's been three weeks since I last saw him at the Talloways' apartment in Paris and for some reason it feels like three months. I shift my feet and glance around the room.

"I can't believe it," I hear him say. I meet his eyes and see a look of mingled amusement and astonishment.

"You're nervous," he says incredulously. "You're actually nervous."

I don't deny it. Our roles have changed now. At least his has. While I'm lucky to still have a job in the CIA, he is no longer the unwanted, uninformed Vice President relegated to the far corner of Lewis's house. He now has The Office. *He* is the man in charge now. As a matter of fact, he could dismiss me from my current job outright if he really wanted to. He's the only other person who knows about Assignment A5367.

"You asked to see me?"

His eyes tell me he's aware of my evasiveness but he doesn't say it.

Instead, he stuffs his hands in his pockets, looks down at his feet and glances back up at me.

"I have an offer for you."

I wait. He continues.

"As you and most of America know, I've cleaned house. Fired every last person who was in Lewis's administration."

"Even your own staff?"

He nods, regret shining in his eyes. "I found them new placement, but yes, I had to get rid of them too. The nation's suspicion of me as their new leader might lessen if I have a completely different administration."

I frown at that and forget my nerves.

"The nation doesn't distrust or suspect you of anything." I tell him. "You're credited as one of the people who brought Operation Windstrom to light. You're the only one who was openly cooperative with the DOJ. The nation trusts you. They *know* that you are a man of integrity."

I blink at my own words and the fire behind them. At some point, I crossed the line between trying to reassure him of his good standing with the nation and admitting my personal view of his character. I keep my mouth shut and look back down at my feet. I look back up when he speaks.

"Thank you," he says. "Thank you for that."

He sighs and runs a hand through his now shortly-cropped hair. It's dark blond and suits him.

"I needed that," he says.

I smile.

"I need you."

I frown.

He crosses the room to stand right before me. "I have an offer for you. Chief of Staff."

My eyes widen and my mouth drops.

I stammer out, "Are you crazy?"

He nods, "I am about a lot of things but not about this. I need people around me whose judgment I can trust. Whose ethics are similar to my own. Do you want to know why I never told Bauer about your ties with Nicolette?"

I'm all ears.

"It was because you did the right thing. You helped her and put yourself at risk to do it. I wasn't about to penalize you for sticking to your convictions; doing the same thing I would have done had I been in your shoes."

I look at him in wonder. "How are you able to keep such optimism after years of politics?"

"I have a friend in high places."

I frown at that. "What place is higher than the presidency?"

"He's in a different Kingdom altogether."

I frown again, not understanding. What nation is more powerful than the United States? China is getting there but it still doesn't compare. He reads the confusion on my face and shakes his head.

"You'll understand someday. You'll understand sooner if you join my team."

I shake my head. "I can't accept it."

"Why not?"

"Because I'm not a politician. I hate politics."

"That's precisely why I want you. You won't B.S. me, especially since you have nothing to hide now. Right?"

He is right and he managed to shred my argument in one second flat but I still shake my head.

"I have a job here."

He nods. "According to Bauer, you're one of the fastest-rising agents in the history of the CIA. But let's admit it, you don't enjoy clandestine work."

I frown. "Is that what he said?"

Lee nods. "He could see it as clearly as I could. Just because you're excellent at a job doesn't mean you're meant to do it. Noelle, this could be a really good fit for you."

I blink at his use of my given name. He didn't use it when Bauer was present. He seems to only use it when we're alone. I can't do this. I don't realize that I'm shaking my head until he speaks again.

"What is it now? Why else can't you take the job?"

"You know why."

He steps closer, only a breath's space away and I have to crane my neck to look up at him. Our eyes lock and for a moment, he lets his guard down. He mirrors back to me everything I've felt but haven't verbalized in the months we've known each other. I know he can see it in my eyes. I don't let my guard down because it was never up to begin with. He raises a hand and stokes my cheek with his thumb. He steps closer, right up to me. I can feel his cool breath brush across my forehead. If he moves just one more inch, our lips will collide. My chest heaves and my heart pounds within it.

I want it. And so does he. His eyes search my own, asking for permission.

I deny it.

I step back, away from his hand, and quietly ask, "Is this why you're making the offer? Is there another offer you had in mind to go with it?"

He closes his eyes as his face flushes red. I'm on the cusp of taking back everything I said regarding his integrity and he knows it. When he opens his eyes, I can guess what he's about to say.

"I'm sorry," he says, his voice surprisingly deeper. He clears it and continues. "I'll admit it. My motives aren't completely pure. I do find you very attractive but my reason for offering you this job has nothing to do with how I feel about you. The White House Chief of Staff is called "The Gatekeeper" for a reason. Whoever I choose will be working closely with me and I need somebody I can trust, who doesn't have their own agenda in mind."

He raises his eyes to me and I see the candor in them.

"I will not disrespect or harass you in any way, shape, or form. If you accept this job, this will be the last time we speak about this."

I nod, his words confirming to me what he just said. If he was serious enough about me to pursue me personally, he wouldn't have put this job offer ahead of a potential relationship. And for that reason, I know that any feelings I've had towards him far outweigh whatever feelings he claims to have for me. It would never have been serious if we'd explored it.

So now I can breathe.

I stretch out my hand and shake his.

"I accept."

2:00 AM – Paris, France

Nicolette:

For reasons unknown to me, my mind is torturing me. At least when I'm awake I can control it. In my sleep, memories come, unbidden and unbridled. Unrestrained, it plays out like a movie in my mind, cutting to the most painful parts of what happened…

"Nicolette, listen to me." Jason pleads.

His use of my given name snaps my eyes to his. He manages to meet my eyes even as the barrel of the gun presses into his skull. His dark blue eyes beg me to listen. He grimaces through the pain, the sight of it heightens my anger.

And my fear.

"You can still make it," he says. "I want you to go without me."

"No," I reply. It's not happening.

"Nic, don't argue with me. Just do it."

The scene cuts and fast forwards—

Jason's body falling into the water.

It cuts again—

Me in the water, looking around for him. Any trace of him.
Red. The only color I can see.
His blood.

He's gone.

I shoot up in my bed, panting for breath. The door to the room opens and the light suddenly flickers on. The torture session of the night is over. For now. My brother walks in and sits on my bed. He wordlessly pulls me into his arms and I allow his familiar scent to comfort me. His hug is masculine, his arms are strong. He's almost the size Jason was and it jars me to find myself comparing the two. I pull back and he lets me go.

"Another nightmare," he says. It's not a question.

His middle of the night entry is a new routine we've established. I toss and turn and make God-only-knows what type of noises, wake up with my heart pounding and my body drenched in sweat. He comes in, turns on the light, pulls me into a hug, and keeps me company until I can fall asleep again. Natalia makes use of her fancy earplugs and has left the job of comforter to our dear brother. To her credit, she did join him the first three nights it happened before resolving that she really did need a full night's sleep for work the next morning.

The dreams usually hit me only once in the night. I don't know what it is, but as soon as Nate and I talk, I'm nightmare-free for the rest of the night.

"I'm okay, Nate." I finally say when my breathing is under control. "You can't keep doing this."

He waves it off the way he always does and continues to stare at me. I meet his eyes unwaveringly.

"Are you ever going to tell me what they're about?"

I shake my head. It's one thing to be tortured by my dreams, it's another to invite them in my real life. I don't need to live them again.

He nods, understanding my refusal.

"Besides this," he gestures to our situation. "How have you liked it here so far?"

I nod. "It's beautiful. Sion is generous."

I'm not just saying that to say it. The French president has been very kind to me and my siblings. My sister is a working journalist but there's no way she could have afforded this apartment on a newbie's salary. And I know she's smart enough not to blow her and Nate's portion of our parent's inheritance to rent such an extravagant place. Either her ties to Sion increased her salary or he managed to hook her up with a very sweet deal on this luxurious ode to minimalist chic.

"Do you trust him?" Nate asks me.

"Do you?" I ask right back.

He shrugs. "He hasn't given me reason not to. At least not yet."

He gets off the bed and excuses himself. "I'll be right back."

He leaves the room and I mull over his answer. I understand his logic but personally disagree with it. Whether or not Sion has done anything suspicious or remotely dishonest is irrelevant. Carter hadn't done anything and neither had Lewis…until they did. It's the first blow that's usually the deadliest. But I won't say anything to Nate. His optimism encourages me. Seconds later, he re-emerges with a tall mug in hand and the scent of hot cocoa wafting in the air.

I smile at him.

"Your favorite, right?" he asks.

I nod and accept the hot drink. "You remembered. Thank you."

"My pleasure," he says. And I know he's not just saying it. Nate actually *likes* to serve others. I can tell it brings him joy. He's a far better Christian than I. Hopefully I'll pick up a thing or two.

I sip at the drink and the warmth of the liquid fills my stomach, radiates to my chest, and tingles my toes. Even more comforting than the drink is the gesture Nate made in giving it to me. I look up at him watching me and suddenly ask what's on my mind.

"Why are you doing this? You're my brother and we love each other, yes, but why all of this?"

Enjoying serving is one thing but I sense there's a deeper reason he feels called to do this. His eyes hover between surprise and bemusement. For a second, they look almost hurt. But finally, his expression settles on one of amusement at my blunt question and he answers, after thinking his response through.

"You never mourned."

The words throw me off. I frown at him.

"What?"

"You never mourned." He meets my eyes, his own a sincere blue.

He explains, "You lost Jason in the middle of a high-powered, high-risk altercation and didn't even get the chance to lay him to rest."

The words pierce my heart. I sip some more of the chocolate, attempting to comfort myself.

"You lost your husband but were too busy running to process it all, much less grieve. These dreams that you're having...I know it's a part of that process. I don't know how long it's going to take, but I'm here for you, Nikki. I want to help you grieve well."

A love I cannot contain for the young man sitting before me overwhelms me and for the first time in weeks, tears spring to my eyes. I pull Nate to me and hug him tightly. My little brother is now a man, a man who sees and understands far more than I've given him credit for.

He hugs me back tightly and whispers in my hair. "It's okay. You're safe now, Nikki."

I pull back, meet his eyes, and shake my head.

"I'm safe *for now*, Nate. There's a difference."

And for now, that'll just have to do.

Rough hands shove at my shoulders and legs. I can hear men yelling near my ear in *Sinhala* - half talking to me, half communicating with each other.

"Hello? Hello, can you hear us?"

"Yes, he's coming to. Don't let him fall back."

"Bring him out of it. He's been out for weeks."

"Wake up, young man. Wake up!"

The hands get rougher. My heavy lids start to lift. The light is almost blinding. It hurts at first but they continue to push me into awareness.

"Keep opening," they yell in *Sinhala. "Keep them open!"*

I obey their commands and blink hard to face the light. I see three shadowed faces hovering over me and realize the light could have been even worse had their heads not blocked it. When my eyes have opened fully, a few of the men clap. I look around. I'm on what appears to be a little cot surrounded by an outdated EKG machine and various medical equipment. The men are dressed in varying uniforms - one in hospital scrubs, the other in a white lab coat similar to what I've worn, and the remaining in what appears to be a police uniform. The latter grabs my attention in Sinhala.

"Welcome back, my friend. You've been unconscious for quite some time. The doctors are going to assess your condition but before they start, we need to know your name."

I look at them for a moment, processing the words. Then it all floods back to me. The beach, the chase, the bridge, my wife's fear-filled eyes, and the dark murky river I remember falling into when I was last conscious. The men push and shove at my shoulders once more and I notice the weakness in my arms, the pain in my left shoulder, the soreness in my legs.

"Sir, your name."

"What is your name?"

"Who are you?"

I shake myself to and look at their inquisitive, though pushy, faces. Still disoriented, I answer in English.

"Jason," I choke out. "My name is Jason Monroe."

To Be Continued...

The story isn't over! Don't miss the exciting conclusion to the story of Nicolette, Jason, and Noelle in the *Type N* trilogy finale: *Trusting No One*.

Sign up to Michelle's newsletter at www.tinyletter.com/mnomedia and be the first to know when it comes out!

No junk. No spam. Only notifications of new releases.

Author's Note

Dear Reader:

I want to thank you for taking the time to read *Taking Names*. It is my hope that you were able to suspend disbelief and escape into the lives of Nicolette and Noelle as they both navigated extremely challenging circumstances. I know I ended the book on a huge cliffhanger and want to assure you that the final book in the *Type N trilogy*, entitled *Trusting No One* will be released next year. It will tie up all the loose ends so make sure you sign up to my newsletter at www.tinyletter.com/mnomedia so that you can be the first to know when this book comes out (and take advantage of some exclusive discounts).

As stated on the copyright page, the U.S. intelligence world referenced in the book is entirely fictitious and has nothing to do with the real workings of any of the agencies and offices mentioned. This follow up wouldn't have been written if it weren't for the numerous requests of readers like you. I want to thank you for having an open mind and taking the time to escape into this work, regardless of your spiritual background. Certainly, some may find spiritual references offensive – especially if they are not ambiguous but I am a believer and I am a writer; I will check neither aspects of my identity at the storytelling door.

I hope you enjoyed the story and I do hope **you'll take the time to write a review and let me and other readers know what you thought of the book.** Unless you're J.K. Rowling, the royalties from a book don't mean nearly as much as the feedback of the person who took the time to read it.

Please also stay in touch. Join my Facebook page to stay in the loop (www.facebook.com/authormichelleonuorah). If you want to be notified of new releases, go to http://tinyletter.com/mnomedia Please also feel free to explore my other work via my Amazon page or my website: www.mnomedia.com.

Also, if you are a non-believer and are curious to learn more about Christ, please feel free to visit my website or contact me directly. I am more than willing to share.

Sincerely,
Michelle

P.S. **The MNO Media Challenge**: Stories are powerful. If you liked this novel and think that others would benefit from reading it, regardless of their background, please consider the MNO Media Challenge by

a.) writing a review on Amazon, Goodreads, and Barnes & Noble

b.) recommending it to people in your inner circle – family and friends

c.) purchasing copies of this book and other MNO Media titles as a gift for others. Stories can impact lives and with your help, a bigger impact can be made. Thanks!

Remember Me

CHAPTER ONE
Prologue

January 1st

"Ahh - get it! Get it, Caleb!"

The little boy with butterscotch skin quickly shot his rifle at the Terminator advancing towards his mother's video game character. He smiled up at his mom and watched in awe as she shot several other terminators in quick succession, all with a look of sheer excitement on her face.

"Take that, you evil monster! Ooh, a grenade!" Kristen aimed her remote at the gaming weapon and loaded up for the journey ahead. As she and her son played the Terminator Salvation video game, everyone else at Chuck-E-Cheese disappeared to them. They had laser focus on the screen in front of them, not even realizing their game had attracted the attention of several kids as well as parents.

Mark smiled as Kristen shot exuberantly at the screen. His wife always did have a way of garnering attention - whether it was at Chuck-E-Cheese or the studio at ABC. His smile dimmed a bit. It was a bitter reminder of her upcoming trip, scheduled only two days after their son's birthday.

She'll be fine, he tried to tell himself. *She's traveled before for special reports. She'll be careful and will return to us in four days. She'll be fine... But did it have to be Afghanistan of all places? Lord, please keep her safe.*

So deep in his thoughts was he that he nearly jumped at the feel of her arms wrapping around his waist.

"You okay?" Kristen asked in concern. He looked down at her and smiled.

"Yeah, I'm fine."

Kristen knew he was lying. She could tell when he was worried even when he tried his best to hide it. And she knew it was because of her upcoming trip. There were numerous things she loved about her job as a reporter - traveling used to be one of them. Now, it was becoming a dreaded aspect of her popular news show. She had traveled to all of Western Europe, much of Eastern Europe, India, China, South America, several nations in Africa from her ancestors' Nigeria to Tanzania, and even North Korea. She knew it was a rare privilege to say she had visited most of the world; but as she got older and her family grew larger, she knew that it was taking a toll on them all, particularly her husband.

She looked up at him and openly admired his chiseled jaw. Mark was tall, lean, and strikingly attractive. At six feet, four inches, he had a body that could easily bulldoze over anything in its path but he was graceful in all of his movements. He had thick dark brown hair that matched his dark brown eyes and his face was arranged with such symmetry and precision that Kristen often thought *Lord, you did good.*

His brows were creased in a worried frown again.

"Honey-"

"Mom, can we go now?" an impatient teenage voice asked. At fifteen, Jasmine was horrified at the idea of spending part of her holiday at Chuck-E-Cheese. When they'd first adopted her at six-years-old, she couldn't get enough of the place; but she had long since outgrown the center and was beyond done with the screeching children running around in obnoxious circles. Mark and Kristen looked at their eldest and were surprised to see that she had already read through the second novel she brought to the party. It had been three hours since they first arrived and they too were ready to leave.

"It's up to your brother," Mark said. "It's his birthday party."

"He's ready to cash his tickets," Jasmine replied.

"And Kylie?"

"YEAH!!!!"

All three heads whipped over to Kylie's exuberant cry. Worried expressions quickly dissolved into shock as they watched their four-year-old daughter jump up and down in the pile of tickets that flowed freely from the "lottery" machine. Caleb rushed up to them.

"Kylie won! She won ten thousand tickets!"

Kristen surmised, "Yeah, I think she's ready to cash hers out too."

The ride home was a happy one. Mom, Dad, brother and sisters couldn't stop chattering about Kylie's good fortune. The little girl was still grinning from ear to ear as she held tightly to the new Barbie doll her tickets had afforded her. The Barbie house and car were sitting in the trunk. Caleb was admiring the G.I. Joe his sister had been kind enough to get for him. Jasmine was busily recalling the look of horror on the management's faces at the sight of all those tickets…and the merchandise they had had to cough up in return.

"Mom, do you have to go?" Caleb suddenly asked.

Kristen sighed. It was the elephant in the car, and the house, and the party that everyone had tried to ignore. It was getting bigger each day her date of departure drew closer. For some reason this particular location was causing triple the anxiety. She glanced at her husband's profile and saw a muscle tick in his jaw. He kept his eyes on the road. She looked back at her three "babies" scrunched together with saddened expressions.

"We've gone over this, you guys. I'll be back in less than a week."

"But why does it have to be Afghanistan?" Jasmine asked, echoing Mark's earlier thoughts.

"That's where the wa—" she caught herself at Caleb and Kylie's expressions, "—the story takes place. It makes no sense for me to go to a different location if the story isn't happening there."

"I thought the war was ending." Jasmine said, refusing to censor herself for her siblings. Her mother glared at her but answered nonetheless.

"It is - which is why we're going. To give updates on how that's moving along and how the troops that are still there are doing."

She could see the concern etched on every single face in the car.

Kylie's small voice piped up, "Can we pray about this?"

"Again?" Kristen asked.

"Why not?" Jasmine countered. "You can never pray too much."

Kristen caught Mark grinning out of the corner of her eye.

She shrugged. "Touché. All right, let's pray."

She reached out her hands and watched as the kids linked up and bowed their heads. Mark kept his eyes on the road but glanced back at the rear view mirror, listening closely to his wife's prayer. When she finished her thoughts, each child took their turn and asked the Lord to protect their mother. They finished with a resounding "Amen!" and Kristen turned back around in her seat.

"Mom?" Caleb asked softly. She turned to him again. "You promise you'll be back soon?"

She smiled and said, "I promise."

Mark drove with one hand on the wheel and reached over to his wife's lap. He gently squeezed her leg before finding her hand and holding it in his own. She smiled at him and met his eyes. Their children had no idea what had just passed between them but it was the agreement of two lovers who were eager for their kids to go to bed.

Thankfully, they didn't have to wait long. The adrenaline of the win began to wear off and the birthday boy, exhausted from running around Chuck-E-Cheese, was soon ready for bed. Kylie's eyes were already drooping and Jasmine had resolved to get her "beauty sleep."

The minute Kristen securely tucked in their youngest, Mark took hold of her waist and swooped her up in his arms like a hat box. Kristen laughed.

"Wow, someone is eager tonight."

"You have no idea."

Fully satiated, Mark rolled over onto his back and pulled Kristen into his side.

"How long are you going to be gone?" he complained. She chuckled and stroked his chest softly.

"It's only four days. I'll be back before you know it."

CHAPTER TWO
Loss

March 15th – Two Months Later

Somewhere in the land between consciousness and slumber, Mark smiled, eyes closed, as he reached out to her side. He turned over as if to capture her beneath his arm and then woke up with a start at the feel of empty sheets.

He was awake.

The smile disappeared as he opened his eyes to the confirmation of what was not there. On the nightstand next to his wife's side of the bed stood the lone photograph of her in her wedding dress, smiling into the camera with a look of sheer joy. He reached out and pulled the frame to him. He caressed the lines of her cheek, the curve of her eyebrows with the very tips of his large fingers. It had become a sort of ritual to him; a way to comfort himself every time he woke up to the reminder that she wasn't there.

He sat up in bed, his hands still clinging to the frame. He glanced at his own nightstand and grimaced. The cards were stacked neatly in the order received, all from family and friends. He had yet to open the cards from the President, other dignitaries, or any of her fans - most of those were held in storage, waiting for him to retrieve them when he was ready. He looked at her photo again and like clockwork, that horrible day came shooting at him all over again.

The kids were scrambling around the house like that of a crew on a ship. Mark, their captain, issued orders on what chores needed to be done and what chores they could check off as complete.

"Okay, the upstairs bathrooms are done, the living room looks clean, you guys already did your bedrooms, so now we have to tackle the kitchen."

Jasmine groaned. "Oh, that's going to be fun."

"You want it to look nice for Mom, don't you?" Caleb pointed out.

"Let's do it!" Kylie declared with a grin on her chubby cheeks. Mark smiled at his youngest and led the charge.

For the first hour, they ignored the phones. So wrapped up were they in getting the house ready, they completely zoned everything out. But as they stopped to take a break, Mark noticed that the ringing wouldn't stop. He looked at the caller ID as the last call dropped off and saw that the caller had rung three times in a row. He pulled up the log and frowned at several other numbers that had called in repeated succession. Even more disconcerting were the caller names: all of them were from family and friends on both sides; the most frequent call was from the ABC producer in charge of Kristen's reporting special: Lance Carson.

He dialed Lance's number, stepped out onto the deck and pulled the phone up to his ear. Lance answered after the first ring.

"Oh, thank God! Mark, is that you?" a panicked Lance exclaimed.

"Yes, it's me. Lance, are you okay?"

There was a moment of silence on the other end.

"Hello?" Mark repeated, "Lance, are you okay?"

"You haven't heard yet," Lance stated in an eerily quiet voice.

Mark's heart dropped. Kristen. He tried to stay calm and kept his voice level.

"Heard what?" he asked. "What happened?"

Suddenly, he heard a rapping on the deck door. He turned around to see his and Kristen's friends, Reed Smith and Dierdra Cole, standing just inside the deck. He frowned at them in confusion. Why were they there?

"Lance, hold on."

He quickly reached the door and pulled it open. Almost immediately, he felt Dierdra enclose him in her arms.

"You haven't told the kids yet. Are you okay?" she asked in near tears.

He looked down at her with a perplexed expression. He glanced at Reed and told them both:

"You guys are scaring me. What happened?"

Their mouths dropped at his question. Mark pulled the phone back to his ear.

"What happened, Lance? Just spit it out."

"It's Kristen," he said without preamble. Mark sat back down on the deck step. "There's been an accident with the crew. Some sort of explosion and we've lost contact with the entire team."

If it was possible to feel all the blood escape from one's heart, Mark felt this was the moment it was happening. He heard a slight ringing in his ears and his palms began to sweat. His breathing was uneven, shallow, and he had to close his eyes to regain any semblance of concentration.

Father, no. Please, no. Not Kristen…

"Mark…?" He lifted the phone back to his ear. "Mark, nothing has been confirmed yet. I just wanted to tell you. Please, keep calm. We're going to get to the bottom of this and find out what is going on. Keep the kids away from the TV."

Mark nodded, although he knew Lance couldn't see him.

"I'll be here," he replied quietly. Lance hung up.

He could feel the eyes of both friends on his back. He stood up on shaky legs and turned to face them. Dierdra's tears had long since fallen. Reed looked at his friend helplessly and said:

"The kids are in Jasmine's room. We got them all to watch a movie."

Mark nodded in appreciation and walked past them into the house again, as though in a trance. He went to the living room, pulled the remote and turned to CNN. In bold letters, the headline appeared:

"KRISTEN TYVERSON AND ABC NEWS CREW MISSING IN AFGHANISTAN EXPLOSION."

Kristen's picture along with various reels of her past reports played on the corner of the screen while in the center, above the headline, footage showed the wreckage of the explosion site. Remnants of a large tankard burned on the wide dirt road as several soldiers and civilians scrambled around it. The reporter reappeared on the screen.

"For those of you just joining us, it has been reported that the vehicle carrying ABC World News *anchor, Kristen Tyverson, and the film crew along with her, has exploded. Tyverson and six members of ABC news team, escorted by two soldiers, were in the middle of surveying civilian sites. Authorities have not released word on the status of any survivors. Details are unclear as to whether all members of the team were in the vehicle. Authorities are still trying to tame the flames and explore the wreckage."*

The ringing returned to Mark's ears as he sat on the coffee table Kristen had chosen for the living room. He was dimly aware of Reed turning off the TV. He barely felt his friend grasp his shoulder. He could barely make out the words in his friend's prayer.

The rest happened in a blur. The same day Kristen was supposed to return home, authorities spent it digging through the wreckage and confirming the deaths of all those aboard. They did not find her body amongst the remains but made an official announcement presuming the deaths of all those who were a part of the reporting team. Accompanied by Lance Carson, two men - one in a military uniform, the other, a police uniform - offered Mark their condolences and left him the last of her effects. Mark would never forget the looks on his children's faces as he told them the news. Each of them responded differently. Kylie wailed in anguish, her small face crumpled in defeat; Caleb ran to his room and refused to open his door for hours. Jasmine quietly cried her grief. With Reed and Dierdra's help, Mark managed to pull them together and comfort them. A week later, they held a private memorial and funeral for Kristen and watched as ABC organized a public, televised memorial.

Present

Mark shook his head and tried to get the images of that time to disappear. It had been more than two months since her passing and he felt the same way he had the minute he'd received Lance Carson's call. He looked down at her portrait. The thought of her body gone, nonexistent, so completely obliterated by a blast that he didn't even have remains with which to bury…

Just two months ago, he had held her in his arms and made love to her. Just five years ago, he had watched her give birth to their daughter. He sometimes wondered if the authorities had been too quick to presume her dead. When he'd first received the notice, he looked for every possible alternative to her being inside of that tankard, especially when they hadn't found her remains. But they had gently reasoned that an explosion like that could vaporize any individual and that some of the crew remains were as little as twenty percent. At her funeral, they arranged a small grave and buried some of her possessions from the trip.

He picked up a card and tore the envelope open. From a distant relative, it simply read Revelation 21:4.

"...and He shall wipe away every tear from their eyes; and there shall no longer be any death; there shall no longer be any mourning, or crying, or pain; the first things have passed away."

A tear slipped down his cheek. And then another. And another. Something rumbled out of his throat from deep within; a cry of loss, loneliness, and shock. He dropped the card and folded the frame to his chest.

Hunching over, he wept.

March 15th - Afghanistan

She woke up with a start. The nurse in attendance had rudely shoved her awake. As Kristen stared up at the Afghan woman ordering her about in her native tongue, Kristen could do nothing but look at her in bewilderment.

"I'm sorry but I don't understand you."

She knows I can't understand a word she's saying. Why does she insist on bothering me before the translator gets here?

To her relief, the young Arab woman in her twenties strode into the ward and spoke to the nurse in their native language. The nurse gave her instructions, glanced at Kristen in annoyance, and left the cot without hesitation.

"Sorry, I'm late," Alima whispered. "How are you feeling?"

"Sore," Kristen replied. "Stiff. Still a bit weak."

"Your muscles have atrophied. Not severely but enough for you to notice a difference."

"How long have I been out again?"

Alima looked at her chart. "You were brought in on the eighth of January. The man who brought you here said you'd been unconscious for a day. You were in a coma from January eighth until February twenty fifth. It's now the fifteenth of March so you've had about three weeks of consciousness."

Kristen remained silent. Alima watched her closely.

"You still can't remember?"

Kristen shook her head.

"Well, you know your name." Alima pointed out. "That's a start. You know where you're from-"

"I just don't know how I got *here*." Kristen interrupted, disturbed. "I've never been to Afghanistan. The only places I've ever been abroad have been in Western Europe. What was I doing here? Where is my family?"

What year is it? Kristen thought the question but was too afraid to ask. She could read the concern in Alima's eyes and knew her memory loss was no joke but she didn't want to know the full extent of it yet. The last thing she remembered was celebrating her job appointment with her mom. She could still remember the disorientation when she first woke up, surrounded by strange faces, all of Middle Eastern descent. The air around her was hot, an arid heat she had never known before; as if it were two seconds away from emitting flames out of thin air. Her muscles had felt weak, her jaw stiff. Even worse, she couldn't speak the language with which the uniformed doctors and nurses were trying to communicate. For the first two weeks, Kristen survived on gestures, paying close attention to the pantomime of her caretakers as they helped her rehabilitate her stiff, wasting muscles. Both sides had learned rudimentary phrases to make the adjustment slightly easier.

When Alima had finally arrived, Kristen had almost cried for joy. But in that time, her presence there had only deepened the mystery. With no identifying documents or personal effects, the local clinic had no idea what to do with Kristen, short of treating her. The mysterious man who brought her in while she was unconscious had disappeared, leaving no contact information behind and Kristen could remember no such man. Even as Alima worked to get her out of the country, a screening process had to be followed, which included confirming her identity and ensuring she was well enough to travel. Given her atrophy and the physical effects from her injuries, the clinic's main priority was to treat Kristen to the best of their ability. That in and of itself was difficult because the clinic had the setup of a 1940s war hospital, with cots lined up back-to-back and no privacy to be found.

Kristen thought of her mom. Alima had tried to contact her via the number Kristen provided but the line was disconnected, confusing Kristen even more.

I need to go home. She'll help me piece the puzzle together.

"I need to get out of here," Kristen said. Alima looked back down at her charts.

"Alima, I've been here for three weeks doing physical therapy. When can I go home?"

"That's the problem, Kristen. I believe that you are an American citizen. You have the accent and everything but we can't find your passport or any evidence that you belong abroad."

Even worse, they could not find records of a "Kristen Johnson" ever having entered the country.

"Then what is the procedure?" Kristen asked.

"There are several documents that need to be processed. It's easier if you have an organization to leave with…which is why I'm having you transferred."

"What?"

Alima smiled. "Surprise. I found a local Red Cross stationed four miles away. They've agreed to take you. You'll have better treatment and an easier time communicating. You won't have to rely on a translations intern to get by. You can also get the travel clearance you need if they approve you."

Kristen closed her eyes in gratitude. She felt weak and drained and she had only woken up a few minutes ago but she was grateful. Grateful that she could soon get out of there and get to the bottom of everything that had happened.

It felt like months to her but five days later, Kristen found herself entering a new medical ward. This one was much cleaner with more space and advanced equipment. There were a variety of patients, mostly local civilians, who were receiving treatment. For once in over three weeks, Kristen was able to communicate seamlessly with several staff members, all of whom spoke English. She noticed that a couple of them took second glances at her and one even froze in astonishment but quickly recovered their expressions. She shrugged off the reactions as simple placement issues. How often do you see an African American woman walking around in Afghanistan in casual clothing? She knew she stood out.

She waited in a makeshift room drawn of nothing but standing curtains. After nearly an hour had passed, the curtain drew back and in walked a tall man with light brown hair and friendly blue eyes; those eyes became saucers the minute he saw her. His eyes swept over her in shock.

"I can't believe it," he whispered. "You survived. You actually survived."

She frowned at his familiar tone. "You know me?"

He nodded and said with a slight frown, "Reed Smith. Friend of the family."

She frowned at this but didn't argue. She had never met him before but she knew her mom had several friends she hadn't been introduced to yet.

"I'm a Red Cross medic out here for a mission. I honestly didn't believe them when they said you were here. Kristen, everyone had presumed you dead."

"My family thinks I'm dead?" Kristen asked.

"There was a funeral service and everything. How did you survive it?"

"Survive what?"

"The bomb. I'm assuming you were near it when it went off."

"That would explain the coma."

He looked down at her chart and nodded, finally understanding.

"I see you have some memory issues."

She nodded. "I know who I am and where I'm from. I just don't remember how I got here."

Reed nodded. "With an explosion at that close range, it's a miracle you're alive, much less with most of your memory intact. It's normal not to remember the moments leading up to your accident."

His mouth was poised to ask another question when the curtain ripped open and a young medic appeared.

"Excuse me," he told Kristen. He turned to Reed. "You're needed in ward four. Emergency amputation."

Reed immediately stood up. He promised Kristen he would return. Several hours elapsed before he did and by then, they only had time for a brief conversation. He initially wanted to contact her family and alert them of her safety but Kristen, in a burst of spontaneity, begged him not to.

"Are you crazy?" he asked. "Kristen, your family has been mourning your death for months. Don't you want to put them out of their misery?"

Her family consisted of her mother and distant relatives she had only met once in a blue moon. *He must mean my mom and close friends,* she thought. Well, as far as she was concerned, her friends could wait. Her mom, she wanted to surprise. She could only imagine the look on her face when she realized her daughter was actually alive. So she insisted and eventually, Reed complied.

In five days' time, though they barely spoke to each other between his other responsibilities and her physical therapy, Reed managed to arrange for Kristen's travel clearance. They left together in a Red Cross-appointed helicopter, returning to the States without any fanfare or struggle. When they arrived on U.S. soil, Kristen allowed Reed to do all of the paperwork and all of the talking. Landing on a private airfield helped the process immensely.

CHAPTER THREE
Reunited

March 20th

Kristen could hardly contain the excitement coursing through her body. After her ordeal, she was relieved to finally see the familiar surroundings of Atlanta, Georgia. As Reed drove past the city structures and into the suburban part of town, she began to imagine the expression on her mother's face when she realized that she was alive. Sure, she'd probably smack her once she learned of how long Kristen had kept it a surprise and she would probably call her daughter out for being so selfish but Kristen couldn't help but see for herself the shock and relief that would cross her mother's face.

Kristen thought it odd that they were driving into Buckhead – the most affluent part of town. Did he have to make a stop before taking her home? Reed entered a quiet subdivision that she didn't recognize but it wasn't until he pulled up to a large, brick-front house that Kristen voiced her confusion.

"Where are we?"

Reed looked at her, a slight look of confusion crinkling his eyes.

"Your home." Before she could respond, he slid out of the car and opened her door.

"Come on, let's see your family."

They made it half way across the lawn before the door burst open and a tiny, little biracial girl sprinted out of the house and into Reed's arms.

"Uncle Reed!"

"Kylie! How's my little munchkin?" But Kylie had stopped listening. She froze stock still in Reed's arms as she looked over his shoulder. An older biracial girl in her teens crossed the threshold, a look of irritation and worry mingled on her face.

"Kylie, how many times have I told you not to just burst out of the hou-"

She stopped mid-sentence, staring at Kristen, eyes wide. A shorter boy with cafe-au-lait skin appeared beside her.

"Mom?"

Kylie had recovered. She shoved herself out of Reed's arms, landed on her feet and sprinted over to Kristen.

"Mommy!"

The boy and teenage girl quickly followed. They embraced her as if she were life itself. Kristen stood still as the children invaded her space and grabbed at her waist.

Kristen frowned at Reed in confusion and Reed's smile slowly disappeared. Why was she reacting this way? He looked closer at her and the realization slowly started to take shape.

"What's going on out here?" a deep, baritone voice called out. The teen pulled back from Kristen a fraction of an inch and turned to the brown haired, brown-eyed man at the threshold.

"Dad, she's alive. She's alive!"

But he had already registered that. A look of complete astonishment was written on his handsome face as Mark crossed the lawn. He didn't know that his feet were running. He didn't know that Reed stood on the lawn. He could barely register the tears that blurred his vision and ran down his cheeks.

His children parted slightly from their mother's form as he reached her and drew her tightly into his arms - so tightly, she felt as though her ribs were about to break. His hands reached up to cup her face as he bent down and kissed her soundly on the lips. Only when she yanked back, eyes wide, did he and those around him snap out of it.

Kristen looked at the people in front of her in horror before turning her gaze to Reed's.

"Where is my family? *Who are these people?*"

Like the sample?
Find out what happens next by ordering *Remember Me.*
Available Online

Check out these other titles by Michelle N. Onuorah:

About the Author

Michelle N. Onuorah is the bestselling author of *Type N*, *Remember Me, Double Identity*, and *Wanna Be on Top?* Originally from Maryland, Michelle grew up with a love of storytelling. She wrote down some of her stories in a notebook and continued to write for fun. At the tender age of thirteen, she wrote her first book, *Double Identity*, and got it published the next year. For three years, she ran an independent magazine, *MNO*, and served as the main writer and editor-in-chief. In 2009, Michelle won the *Captured Moments Creativity Award* for her poem entitled *Encounter*. Her writing has appeared in *Vestiges Literary Magazine, Avalon Literary Review*, and *Medium.com* among others. Michelle also enjoyed a successful career as a model in her teens, walking down runways during New York Fashion Week. In August of 2013, Michelle broke several of Amazon Kindle's Bestsellers lists for her debut novel, *Type N*. The following year, she enjoyed another bestseller with the well-loved novel, *Remember Me*. A graduate of Biola University, Michelle continues to write and publish under her company, MNO Media, LLC (www.mnomedia.com). You can learn more about Michelle at that website as well as like her page at www.facebook.com/authormichelleonuorah. Those interested in being notified of her new releases can go to www.tinyletter.com/mnomedia.